"This is a bad idea."

"Why?" Helen asked, her voice brave.

"Because I'll be gone tomorrow," Rafferty replied. "And you'd be alone, figuring you'd been a fool."

"No. I wouldn't." Helen sat up, slowly. "Don't you know that people spend a lot more time regretting the things they don't do, and not the things they do?"

"Helen, you're not the type for a one-night stand. You're the kind of woman who needs commitment, who needs tenderness and a future. I can't give you any of that."

"Why am I trying to talk you into this?" she asked. "Isn't it supposed to be the other way around?"

He made himself touch her, just to prove that he could, cupping her face with his hands. "Lady," he said, "I'll break your heart."

"My heart, Rafferty? Or is it your own you're worried about?"

"I have no heart, Helen. No heart to break."

"Prove it."

ABOUT THE AUTHOR

Anne Stuart, "the scourge of male bimbos," as she calls herself, likes stories of magic and tales of love that transcend the powers of life and death. She's also more than passingly fond of her "gorgeous husband and two wonderful children, not to mention her dog and four cats."

Books by Anne Stuart

HARLEQUIN AMERICAN ROMANCE

Don't miss any of our special offers. Write to us at the following address for information on our newest releases.

Harlequin Reader Service
P.O. Box 1397, Buffalo, NY 14240
Canadian address: P.O. Box 603,
Fort Erie, Ont. L2A 5X3

Anne Stuart

One More Valentine

Harlequin Books

TORONTO • NEW YORK • LONDON
AMSTERDAM • PARIS • SYDNEY • HAMBURG
STOCKHOLM • ATHENS • TOKYO • MILAN
MADRID • WARSAW • BUDAPEST • AUCKLAND

To Julie Kistler, who provided me with the legal and Chicago-area expertise. Any mistakes are entirely her fault. Love ya, Julie.

This is a work of fiction based on the events of the morning of February 14, 1929, in an old garage in Chicago. The names and lives of the victims have been changed; the details of the massacre are essentially correct.

Published February 1993

ISBN 0-373-16473-4

ONE MORE VALENTINE

Chapter One

Helen Emerson sat bolt upright in bed and screamed. No sooner had the sound vanished in the darkness than she clapped her hands over her mouth, as if to call back the shriek of unbelieving horror. A moment later she groped for the bedside lamp, turning it on, banishing the ghosts into the darkness where they belonged. She drew her hand back and noticed that it was trembling.

She swung her legs over the side of the bed and shook her head. Five-thirty in the morning, and she couldn't remember her dream. Couldn't remember the horrific nightmare that had torn her from sleep, and she wasn't sure she wanted to. A few lingering impressions drifted through the back of her mind. A roaring kind of noise, one she couldn't place. And the sound of a dog barking.

She shook her head and ran a hand through her shoulder-length brown hair. She prided herself on being a practical woman, at least when anyone else was looking, and a nightmare was simply a nightmare.

But this wasn't the first time she'd had it. There was no way to know whether the same dream had haunted her those other times—she simply didn't remember anything about them. But there was a constant—the thunderous noise, like a thousand drumbeats. And the eerie howling of a dog.

Pushing herself off the bed, she tugged her oversize T-shirt down and wandered into her kitchen. She plugged in the coffeemaker, then stared unseeingly at the calendar. Friday the thirteenth. No wonder she was having nightmares.

She stared out into the early-morning light. February had to be the bleakest month of all, particularly in a city like Chicago. The wind whipped off the lake, freezing everyone to the bone, and the whole world seemed gray and desolate. In another month and a half things would start blossoming. For now not even the silly specter of Valentine's Day could lighten Helen's heart.

She couldn't wait for the coffee. She poured herself a cup as the coffee continued to splash down onto the burner, then wandered into the living room of her apartment. She loved this old building, and her apartment in particular. After decades of decay, 1322 Elm Street was finally part of urban renewal, and Helen was doing her part to bring the venerable old place back into shape. It had once been one of the most elegant town houses in Chicago, but years of neglect had taken their toll, until the place had sat derelict, waiting for someone with enough energy and money to save it.

On an assistant prosecutor's salary Helen was hardly possessed of the money, but she had energy to spare. There was no distracting man in her life, no one to bring her valentines and chocolate tomorrow, no one she'd send a card to. She would lavish her love on her funky old building, as always.

No, scratch that. Her brothers would probably send her valentines. They missed the point of the entire celebration. And come to think of it, she'd already mailed valentines to each of her seven nieces and nephews. Maybe she should just forget what February fourteenth stood for and concentrate on chocolate.

At least it was on a Saturday this year. She wouldn't have to deal with all the forced merriment at work, the arch comments, the little games. Besides, she wasn't feeling very jovial about her job right now. Then again, there wasn't much about her job to make a person cheerful. Dealing with criminals wasn't conducive to optimism.

She took another deep sip of her coffee, wondering if there was any way she could get out of going to work today. Call in sick, call in depressed. Everyone needs a mental health day now and then—surely Friday the thirteenth would qualify as a good enough reason. Then she'd have another two days to come to a decision about Billy Moretti.

But she was a responsible woman, and two days wouldn't make any difference. She was a prosecutor, albeit a minor level one, and Billy Moretti had broken the law. It was her job to make sure he paid for it. Even if it felt as if she were kicking a helpless puppy.

She walked through the apartment, turning on every light in defiance of her electricity bill. It was going to be a cold, blustery day, gray and depressing, and she needed all the light she could get. Maybe she'd get to work early, face up to the Moretti case and any other bit of unpleasantness and then escape in the early afternoon. Treat herself to an elegant, late lunch, maybe even go shopping. When the going gets tough, the tough go shopping. Surely she could find something to waste money on. Even if she had to succumb to her shameful weakness for old movies that she could just as easily tape off television.

She drained her coffee, shivering in the cool air, and headed for the bathroom. A long hot shower would clear her head, wake her up, help her face the day. But as she stood under the pelting streams of water, she thought she could hear the thundering drumbeats in the distance. And the mournful howl of a dog.

JAMES SHERIDAN RAFFERTY leaned against the old brick building and closed his eyes. He remembered the first time he'd turned up back here, and the horror that had swept through him. He remembered the time he'd come back to find the garage torn down, rubble in its place.

Damn, he was cold. His feet were freezing, the wind was whipping through his old overcoat and he had no gloves. He shoved his hands into his pockets, shivering, reveling in the physical sensations. He was hungry. He was cold. He was horny.

He opened his eyes, pulling the crumpled piece of paper out of his pocket, the one Mary Moretti had handed him, her eyes wide and pleading. Back in Chicago for only a few hours and his short stay was already tied up.

He shouldn't regret it. He'd always been fond of Billy Moretti. Of all of them, he was the one who least deserved his fate. He was only a kid, and a good one at that. Young enough to make mistakes. Old enough to learn from them, and go on. If he got another chance.

Mary had looked terrified, and no wonder. She was nineteen years old, more than a little pregnant and her husband was looking at some hard time in Joliet prison. The only man she could turn to was James Sheridan Rafferty, and she was frightened of him. Not that he could blame her. He scared a lot of people, a fact that seldom bothered him. It was something about his stillness. Something about his eyes. Something about who he was, that people never quite understood but instinctively suspected. And recoiled from.

Just as Mary Moretti recoiled from him. But not when her beloved Billy was in danger. For Billy's sake she'd face the devil himself if she had to. And he could tell by the panic in her dark eyes that she considered he was a definite candidate for the job of Satan.

How could he tell her no? So what if he only had forty-eight hours in Chicago? Forty-eight hours into which he had to cram an entire year of living? He was learning responsibility, even if it was taking decades to sink in. He was learning to care about the other guy. Billy had stood by him, more times than he could remember. He had no choice but stand by him.

He glanced down at the piece of paper, written in Mary's spidery handwriting. Helen Emerson. Assistant State's Attorney.

He shook his head. He could never get over that. A woman prosecutor. Hell, she might even have a male secretary. The world had gotten screwy.

He took a cigarette from the crumpled pack in his coat pocket and lit it, cupping his hands around the wooden match to keep it out of the wind. His first cigarette in a year, and it tasted wonderful. That was another problem—each year fewer and fewer people smoked. It got so he couldn't find a place to light up without someone glaring at him, giving him a lecture about the state of his lungs. He'd usually listen in stony politeness, and the crusader would taper off, unnerved by his stillness.

One thing was for certain, he couldn't get on with his plans for the next forty-eight hours until he saw what he could do about Billy. It was six o'clock in the morning—Ms. Emerson probably wouldn't make it into work until nine. There was no way he was going to hang around, waiting. Three hours were too big a chunk of time to toss down the toilet.

He was going to find Ms. Helen Emerson and see if she couldn't be reasonable. He had a certain amount of weathered charm if he cared to use it. Surely he could manage to sweet-talk the woman into dropping the charges. Otherwise, he could always resort to giving her an offer she couldn't refuse.

He wished he could just forget about Billy. Enjoy his stay in Chicago with a single-minded pursuit of pleasure, as he had so many other years.

But he was a different man. Time had changed him. And he just couldn't enjoy himself, thinking of Billy stuck away in prison. Thinking of his pregnant, frightened wife. He was going to have to do something about it, and the sooner the better.

The Elm Street address had an uncomfortably familiar ring, one he couldn't place. It was in a part of town that had once been fancier than what he'd been used to. It had gone downhill since then, turning into slums, and he couldn't imagine a lawyer living there, even one on the city payroll. But he should be getting used to surprises by now, and Ms. Helen Emerson having the power of life and death over one Billy Moretti and living on Elm Street was a minor one compared to some of the others.

He took a taxi, counting on the fact that his wallet would still be full. It wasn't until they were pulling up outside a residential street that he leaned forward.

"Hey, buddy," he said to the driver. "What year is it?"

"You kidding?" The cabbie turned around to stare at his passenger in disbelief.

"Nope. Just checking."

"It's 1993, pal. What did you think it was?"

Rafferty smiled thinly. "Sounds about right to me." He tipped the driver, then climbed out onto the sidewalk, staring up at the building as his memory drifted into focus: 1993. And James Sheridan Rafferty had been dead for sixty-four years.

HELEN HEARD THE DOORBELL ring. She slammed her hand against the wall in surprise, then cursed, glad her Irish Catholic father wasn't around to hear her. Her brothers, either, for that matter. Despite the fact that her father and all four of her brothers were cops and used to the foulest language this side of the gutter, they still didn't like to hear their sweet little Helen come out with anything as blasphemous as a "damnation." And Helen prided herself on coming out with words that were a great deal more colorful. She'd learned a lot in the three years she'd worked in the Prosecutor's Office.

Who in heaven's name could be ringing her doorbell at half-past six in the morning? For a moment panic swept through her, as every conceivable family disaster raced through her mind, and it took all her formidable common sense to realize that the telephone would be the obvious medium of communication. If disaster had struck the far-flung Emersons she would have heard about it by now.

She took another hurried gulp of her third cup of coffee, yanked at the recalcitrant zipper of her calf-length skirt and hobbled toward the door, wearing one high-heeled shoe, the other still in her hand. She had three chains and a bar in place, and she peered through the peephole. "Who is it?" she demanded nervously.

She couldn't see much of him, since the peephole was scratched, filthy and ancient. He was tall, and dark, and for all she knew he could be a serial killer.

"My name's Rafferty. You Ms. Emerson?"

She didn't like the faintly mocking emphasis on the word "Ms." She didn't like his voice, rough and smooth at the same time, with a trace of an East Coast accent. "I'm Emerson," she said flatly, yanking on the other shoe and making no effort to open the door. "What do you want?"

"I'd like to talk to you about Billy Moretti."

Great, she thought, leaning against the door. That was all she needed on this rotten, dismal morning. "I'll be in my office at nine o'clock," she said flatly. "See me there."

"Can't do it," his voice drifted back through the heavy door. "I'm only in town for forty-eight hours and I've got a lot of business to accomplish. I tell you what, Ms. Emerson. It's not even seven in the morning—you don't have to be at work for another couple of hours. Let me buy you breakfast, hear me out and then I'll go away."

"And if I say no?" She heard her own words with a start of shock. What in the world did she mean, *if* she said no? Of course she was going to say no. She wasn't going anywhere with the friend of a man she was going to prosecute.

"Then I'll just stay here until you change your mind." He sounded eminently reasonable and completely implacable.

"The police are only a phone call away, Mr. Rafferty. I won't be harassed."

"Lady—" his voice was long-suffering "—trust me, I have no interest in harassing you. I just want to see if we can do a deal about Billy."

She found herself considering it for a moment. The Moretti case had been preying on her mind for days now. If she could just deal with it then Friday the thirteenth would become a lot more pleasant.

"Do you work with Abramowitz?"

"Of course," the voice replied immediately.

That decided her. If Billy's lawyer was gung ho enough to find out where she lived and come over at the crack of dawn, then the least she could do was meet him for breakfast to discuss the case. After all, they were both professionals. It was silly to be formal about it.

"Hold on a moment," she said, fiddling with the locks, her hands clumsy. By the time she got the last one opened and pulled the security bar away she was beginning to regret her hastiness in accepting him, but by then the door was ajar and it was too late. At least she kept the chain in place as she peered through the four-inch space at the man waiting in the hallway.

He stood there patiently enough, and his very stillness was slightly unnerving. He was a tall man, leanly built, and the suit and overcoat he was wearing were nondescript, ageless. His hair was dark, short, combed back from a widow's peak over dark, challenging eyes. She looked into those eyes, into those still, fathomless eyes, and she felt a chill run through her. Followed by a rush of heat.

"You don't look like the type Abramowitz usually hires," she said foolishly. Certainly not the sort to defend the Billy Morettis of this world. He was too handsome, with his wide, sensual mouth, his narrow, high-boned face, his cool, self-contained grace.

He smiled then, and she should have been relieved. It was a charming smile, literally, designed to charm wary females. Helen could feel the tug, and she fought it.

"Looks can be deceiving," he said, his dark eyes running down the narrow length of the door opening. "Are you going to let me buy you breakfast?"

She should slam the door in his face. She could always give Jenkins the Moretti case, as he'd wanted, but Jenkins was a pig and a bully, very hard core and out to make a point, and extenuating circumstances weren't going to matter to him in the slightest.

She stared for one long moment at the man who called himself Rafferty, and then nodded, deciding. She was a smart woman, a careful woman. But she was also a woman who learned to go by her instincts. And her instincts told her to trust this man.

She slid the chain off and opened the door. "Come in," she said, stepping back. "I'll be with you in a minute."

It wasn't until she was halfway across the room, scooping papers into her briefcase, that she realized how very odd her behavior was. She didn't like to let people, particularly co-workers, into her apartment.

For one thing, she was completely disorganized and a borderline slob. For another, yuppies didn't tend to appreciate the 1920s' decor she was striving for. She glanced back at Rafferty, trying to hide her nerves, and then stopped still.

He was standing in the middle of her apartment, a tall, dark stranger who should have been an interloper, and he was staring around him with an air of wonder, and oddly enough, recognition.

"Have you been in this apartment before?" she found herself asking.

His dark eyes met hers, and he smiled, that easy, surface smile. "No," he said.

She didn't believe him. And then she laughed aloud at her own absurdity. "Of course you haven't," she said. "This building was home to a strange old lady and her cats for the last sixty-some years."

"What happened to her?"

"The old lady?" Helen said, pulling on her down coat. "She died, I'm afraid. She was quite a character—legend had it she was an old gun moll from Al Capone's day. I could believe it."

"You knew her?"

Helen shrugged. "I met her through my job. She was mugged. I was the prosecuting attorney for the snake who knocked her down. I think she decided to adopt me." She smiled at the memory. "She was a great old lady."

"What was her name?"

"Her name? It wouldn't mean anything to you—I don't think she'd left this street in the last three decades before she went to the hospital."

"If she really was a gun moll I might have heard of her. I've always been interested in the gangland days in Chicago."

"You and half the city," Helen said. "Her name was Jane Maxwell."

"Never heard of her."

"I believe she went by the name of Crystal Latour. Hard to imagine anyone that old being called Crystal, but that's what she told me."

"Crystal Latour," Rafferty said in an odd voice. "Yeah, it's hard to believe."

She grabbed her briefcase and headed for the door, ignoring her coffee, the newspapers littering the old sofa, the half-eaten bagel on the scarred dining-room table. "Are you ready?"

He seemed to rouse himself from a kind of trance. "Sure thing. I was just wondering how you ended up here."

He was sharp, she had to admit it. He'd honed in on the most uncomfortable facet of this wonderful old place within minutes. She'd hate to meet a man with those kinds of instincts in court. "She left it to me, Mr. Rafferty. The entire building."

"Did she, now? You must have done a hell of a job prosecuting that mugger."

She paused by the door, eyeing him frostily. "I did the same job I do for everyone, Mr. Rafferty. I prosecute criminals."

"Punish the bad guys," he said in a mocking tone of voice. "Make them pay their debt to society."

"I'm not usually into vengeance, though I must admit I've had my moments. I'm more interested in keeping little old ladies like Crystal safe."

He smiled wryly, but that smile didn't reach his dark, still eyes. "And I'm sure you do a terrific job." He glanced around the spacious, untidy room, and it took her a moment to control her irritation. It wasn't her fault that Crystal had left her the building. And it wasn't as if it were any great legacy—the place was in deplorable shape and at least three contractors had told her she'd be better off tearing it down and starting anew.

She couldn't bring herself to do it. She loved the lines of the building, the gracefulness of the past, even buried under adhesive wall covering and linoleum flooring. She was fixing it up bit by bit, as she could afford to, starting with her own first-floor apartment, planning eventually to renovate the upper floors and turn them into rental units. It seemed eminently practical to her. Her brothers told her she was dreaming.

"I thought you came by to discuss the Moretti case, not my domestic arrangements," she said in a deceptively cool voice.

"I did. You know a good place to eat?"

"Not in this neighborhood. Why don't we eat near my office? That way we can clear things up if we come to an agreement. We'll take my car."

"Yes, ma'am," he said.

She cast another suspicious glance at him, wondering if he were mocking her. He was making her feel strange, prim and proper and schoolmarmish. The longer she was with him, the more she wanted to tug her hem down, to wrap her coat around her. He made her uneasy.

"Then let's go," she said brightly. "I've got a lot of work ahead of me." She waited pointedly by the door for him to precede her, and he did after a minute.

"Nice place you got here," he said in that raspy, disturbing voice. He paused in the doorway to look down at her, and he was too close to her. She looked up into his eyes, and noticed that they weren't as dark as she'd first thought. Deep brown, they were lit with tiny flecks of gold, warming their chilly depths. They were eyes one could fall into, eyes that could hypnotize and enchant. Eyes that could seduce.

And then he moved past her, without touching her, heading down the short flight of stairs to the front door. She watched him go, for a moment tempted to run back into her apartment and slam and lock the door behind her. He made her uneasy in ways she couldn't even begin to comprehend.

But if she started running away from shadows her life would quickly deteriorate into disaster. She glanced into her apartment for a moment, imagining how he viewed it. And then she closed the door, following Rafferty out into the early-morning chill.

CRYSTAL LATOUR, Rafferty thought as he slid into the restaurant booth across from Helen Emerson. They'd made it to the center of town in one of those tiny little Japanese cars, half the size of the Packard he used to drive, and his long legs had been squashed. Even that discomfort couldn't distract him from the disturbing memory of Crystal Latour.

He'd been to 1322 Elm Street, all right. Only once, on February 13, 1929. He'd spent the night in Crystal Latour's bed, and the next morning he'd been dead.

He glanced over at the woman. She'd been a surprise, all right. He'd gotten marginally used to modern women, to their cool, self-assured beauty, their independence, their invulnerability. The woman who'd driven her tiny little car with a singular lack of nerve was a throwback.

She was far from invulnerable. All you had to do was look into her huge brown eyes and you could see just about everything that went on in her mind. Her hair was long, a rich shade of reddish brown, her mouth was wide and generous. A good mouth for kissing.

Not that he wanted to kiss her. She was a little too skinny for his tastes, and she dressed like a man. She was doubtless some wild-eyed feminist, with her lack of makeup and her wire-rimmed glasses that looked like something his accountant would have worn. She probably only slept with women.

Except he didn't think so. He wasn't imagining that strange little tug of attraction that was damnably mutual. He didn't want to get involved with Ms. Helen Emerson. He didn't have time to get involved with someone like her during his forty-eight-hour stay.

He needed someone cheerful and easy, someone to
lie down with him and laugh with him and give him
comfort and release. He didn't want commitment or
complications or even friendship, and with a woman
like Helen Emerson you were bound to provide all
three before you even got to touch her breasts. She
probably didn't even have any worth touching.

But damn, he wanted to find out.

"Have you been working for Abramowitz long?"
she asked, glancing at him over the menu with disap-
proval as he lit a cigarette.

"Not long," he said, wondering who the hell
Abramowitz was.

"You don't look like a lawyer," she said.

"You do," he replied with less charm than he usually used. He didn't want to charm her. Because for
some irrational reason he didn't want to lie to her any
more than he absolutely had to.

His reply had been a mistake. She smiled at his
subtle barb, her eyes crinkling, her wide mouth curv-
ing upward. "I do my best," she replied. "So what are
we going to do about Billy Moretti? He's looking at
hard time—probably eight to ten years in Joliet, and
I can get a conviction."

He gave his order to the saintly waitress who poured
him his first cup of coffee in a year and then leaned
back, watching Helen. "Then why am I here?" he
asked, taking a deep drink of the coffee and following it with the cigarette.

"Maybe because I'm curious," she said. "You
don't look like the kind of sleazes Abramowitz usu-

ally hires. And maybe I'm not convinced Billy Moretti deserves to go to prison for that long. Maybe he just made a mistake.''

"You want to define his mistake for me?''

"Don't you know?''

"I'd rather hear your opinion,'' he said coolly.

She was too damned easy to manipulate. She shrugged, agreeably enough. "He was on probation. He has a juvenile record as long as his arm—nothing terribly nasty, but the cumulative effect is impressive. He knew he had to be very very careful, and yet he was caught with firearms, caught in the company of a notorious criminal, caught in the commission of a felony.''

"What felony?''

She looked annoyed as she added too much sugar to her coffee. "You know as well as I do. He was the driver during the Carnahan robbery. A lot of jewelry was stolen from that store, Mr. Rafferty, and the insurance company is out for blood.''

"And what's his story?''

"That he didn't do it. That he just happened to be in the wrong place at the wrong time. Hard to believe when he'd been arrested twice in his youth with the man who masterminded that robbery and half a dozen others.''

Rafferty stubbed out his cigarette. "So why don't you want to throw the book at him, counselor? Why are you willing to deal with me?''

If he'd hoped to intimidate her he'd failed. She simply shook her head. "I don't know, Rafferty. It's a sixth sense you sometimes develop. When you know someone's managed to turn his life around. I thought that was the case with Billy. I still think that's the case with Billy, but I have no proof and he won't talk. Unless I have a reason to look the other way, I'm going to have to throw the book at him."

"You want a reason?" Rafferty said, draining his coffee and thinking fast.

"I want a reason."

"Who's the man who masterminded the robbery?" It was a blind shot, but it worked. She leaned back, thunderstruck, and it took all his effort to keep his face blank, unreadable.

"Of course," she said. "Why didn't I think of that? He's one of the most dangerous men I've ever met. If he decided he wanted Billy to help on the Carnahan robbery then it would be a simple enough matter to make him do it. Threaten his wife, for one thing."

"And his wife is very pregnant," Rafferty pointed out.

"Is she? It makes sense, then. I just need Billy to admit it. We need everything we can get if we're going to stand a chance in hell in catching Morris." She leaned forward, and in her intent gaze she forgot to protect herself. Forgot he was dangerous. "Will he testify?"

"If I have to break his neck," Rafferty said grimly. "When can I see him?"

"We'll head on over after breakfast." She looked at him curiously. "Unless you aren't hungry?"

The waitress arrived at that moment, setting a plate of fried eggs, sausage, bacon, hash browns and steak in front of him. The whole thing was swimming in grease, and he heaved a sigh of anticipatory pleasure. "I'm hungry," he growled.

Helen looked down at her own meager order of toast. "Do you eat that much cholesterol every morning?"

"Every morning I get the chance."

"You'll die young," she said primly.

He leaned back, surveying her from beneath hooded eyes. "You're right," he said. And he began to eat.

Chapter Two

Rafferty never could figure out why jails had a certain smell. Maybe it was the cold sweat of fear, the stink of despair, combined with the faint odor of defiance. Ms. Helen Emerson had her offices on the third floor of an anonymous-looking courthouse, but somewhere in that building were jail cells and holding tanks. He knew it as well as he knew his own name.

Her office was just as cluttered and untidy as her apartment, though the small cubicle looked marginally more modern, complete with something he recognized as a computer and a fancy-looking telephone. He dropped into one of the uncomfortable chairs and breathed a sigh of relief. It had given him quite a turn when he'd first stepped inside her apartment. He'd recognized the place when he'd left the taxi, but he'd grown used to familiar things changing. What had startled him was how close the inside of the apartment was to what he'd remembered. The prim, undoubtedly virginal Ms. Emerson had more in common with the late, great Crystal Latour than she would have ever imagined.

He didn't know why he knew Helen Emerson was a virgin. God knows virginity seemed to be a deservedly outdated concept for the past thirty years, but Ms. Emerson was a throwback. As untouched as the Roman Catholic nuns who tried to beat morality into him when he was a kid.

"I'll have them bring Billy up," she said. "I imagine you'll want to talk to him alone." She pushed a hand through her shoulder-length brown hair. It hung straight around her face, and he wondered how she'd look with a marcel wave. They didn't do that anymore, did they? Besides, maybe he preferred it long and flowing.

"Sure," he said, reaching for his cigarettes. "Do you always wear those glasses?"

She put a startled hand up to her face, almost as if she'd forgotten they were there. "Only when I want to see," she replied tartly.

"What about contact lenses?"

"What about mind your own business, Mr. Rafferty?" she shot back. "And this is a smoke-free building."

He paused, the crumpled pack in his hand. "Smoke-free building?" he echoed in horror. "That's the first I've heard of that. What's coming next—smoke-free cities?"

"If I had anything to say about it," Helen muttered.

He shoved the pack back into his jacket. "Got any laws against gum chewing?" he drawled, pulling the pack that was always in his pocket, untouched, when he returned to Chicago.

"Not at present." She stared at him curiously. "What kind of gum is that?"

He glanced down at the package. They hadn't sold Black Clove since the early thirties—he should have remembered that if he didn't want to answer unanswerable questions.

"You wouldn't like it, counselor," he said, tucking the incriminating package back into his jacket. At least men's clothing styles didn't change much over the years. A dark suit was a dark suit, and if some years the lapels were too wide and other years too narrow, few people had dared to question it. Or him.

"I'll get Billy," she said again, leaving him alone in her office.

He sat very still, his gaze fixed on the dismal Chicago skyline outside her grimy window. Each year it changed, each year new buildings broke the horizon. He'd hated the Sears Tower the most. Still hated it, as a matter of fact. But he didn't want to look around Helen Emerson's office and find out too much about her. Because the more he found out, the more drawn he was to her.

And he had to admit it, irrational or not, he was attracted to her. It didn't seem to matter that she was too skinny, too flat chested and too innocent for him. Not to mention too smart and sassy. He'd always made it his business to steer clear of women like Helen, but fate had conspired against him. And it was damned unfair. Forty-eight hours to spend in Chicago, and he had to waste it on a lost cause like Helen Emerson.

He pulled his gaze away from the city that he no longer knew to glance over at Helen's desk. There was a photograph in a place of honor, one he couldn't avoid seeing. There was Ms. Emerson, dressed in men's clothes again, but at least the skirt she was wearing was short enough to show a quite spectacular pair of legs. She was flanked by no less than five cops—one old man and four younger ones who were so alike they could only be related. There was no denying Helen's resemblance, either—she was a hell of a lot prettier than the five men, but he had no doubt whatsoever he was looking at her father and brothers.

Just his luck, he thought wearily. He'd been forced to cozy up to a lawyer, only to find she had half the Chicago police force in her family.

"Rafferty?" Billy's scared young voice broke through his abstraction.

Rafferty turned swiftly, searching Billy's face for signs of abuse, of bruising. He looked nothing more than scared.

He crossed the room and hugged him, hard, before releasing him. "You look okay, kid," he said gruffly. "They didn't hurt you?"

Billy shrugged. "The coppers aren't like they used to be, Rafferty. They don't work you over unless they've got a good reason. That, or if you happen to live in L.A."

"You lost me."

Billy shook his head. "It doesn't matter. Rafferty, we've got trouble..."

"You mean *you've* got trouble," Rafferty corrected. "How the hell did you get picked up? You were always too smart for that."

Billy sighed, slumping down in the chair Rafferty had vacated. He wasn't even twenty-five yet, a raw-boned, sweet-natured boy who'd gotten more trouble than he'd deserved all those years ago. Rafferty thought he'd had everything taken care of when he left last time. Apparently he was mistaken. "It wasn't my fault," Billy began.

"That's what they all say," Rafferty shot back. He'd given this lecture so many times in his and other men's lifetimes that he knew it by heart. "Do you know that your wife's scared to death?"

Billy's face paled, and he jumped from the seat. "What happened? Did anyone touch her? Is she okay, is the baby...?"

"Relax, Billy." Rafferty shoved him back into the chair. "She's fine. How did you think I found out where you were? She came to me."

Billy shook his head. "You're right, she must be really scared, if she was willing to talk to you about it."

"I don't know what you've told her to terrify her so much...." Rafferty said in a weary voice.

"It's nothing I've said. She just looks at you."

"Great," Rafferty growled. "She needs you home, Billy. She needs you not to make dumb mistakes like getting involved with a criminal when you're already on probation. You've been keeping your nose clean for the past two years—what in God's name made you decide to throw your lot in with a creep named Morris? Were you worried about having enough money for the baby?"

For a moment Billy just looked at him. Then he shook his head. "It's not that, Rafferty. God knows, I'd do anything to give my wife and baby a good life, but I figured having a husband and dad around was better than risking it all on a bankroll."

"Then why did you get involved with someone like Morris?"

Billy glanced around the room. "This place bugged?"

"Who the hell cares?"

"I do. If I tell the cops he'll find me and cut my throat. Mary's, too. And he's the man to do it."

"Is that why you agreed to drive the car? That's Ms. Emerson's theory, by the way. I don't ascribe to it— I'm keeping an open mind."

Billy allowed himself a brief, humorless laugh. "That Ms. Emerson's something, all right. She had me pegged from the word go. She's too damned smart. But I didn't tell her."

"Didn't tell her what?"

"About Morris."

"What about Morris?"

Billy turned his head to stare out at the dismal landscape. "He said he'd kill Mary if I didn't help him," he said in a low, toneless voice. "And he would have. You remember what it was like, Rafferty. They put out the word, and it gets done. There's no place you can hide from them.''

"This isn't Chicago in the 1920s, Billy,'' Rafferty said, ignoring the little chill of apprehension that ran up his spine. ''No one has the nerve to do the sort of thing the gangs did back then.''

"Except Morris. He would have killed her. And he would have enjoyed it.'' He met Rafferty's gaze. ''And you know why, Rafferty?''

He wasn't absolutely sure he wanted to know. ''Why don't you tell me?'' he said, wishing like hell he had a cigarette.

"Because Willie Morris wasn't always Willie Morris. He used to be known by another name, back in the old days. He's Drago, Rafferty. Ricky Drago. And he's totally out of his mind.''

For a moment Rafferty didn't move. And then he very calmly reached into his coat pocket, pulled out his cigarettes and lit one. ''Hell,'' he said briefly, taking a deep drag. ''Hell and damnation.''

IT HAD NEVER MADE ANY sense to a man like Jamey Rafferty. Maybe that was why he kept returning, year after year, why he couldn't simply let go and try to accept the way things were.

He'd had more brains than the other six men put together, the other six men who'd died in that Chicago garage on St. Valentine's Day more than sixty years ago. That had been his value to Moran, his brains, not his brawn. Moran was someone who knew how to use his human tools—the Scazzetti brothers were simple enforcers, with limited brainpower and unlimited brawn. They made the collections, guarded Moran and made certain no one thought they could get away with anything.

Then there was Richstein and von Trebbenhoff, two middle rank dons from the outlying areas, who just happened to be in Chicago on that fateful day. Neither of them were complicated men—they did what they were told and didn't ask questions. Billy Moretti was a kid, a messenger boy, someone who lived on the fringes of the gang and was well paid for it. He had a widowed mother and three sisters who counted on him, and Billy was willing to take chances for their sakes.

And then, of course, there was Ricky Drago. He was a killer, pure and simple, one who took pleasure out of blood and terror. They had a lot of fancy names for people like him nowadays: sociopath, mass murderer, monster. People like Drago came along once in a generation. Unfortunately it looked as if Drago was getting a second chance.

The other six had accepted their fate without a lot of questions. They'd met death in that Chicago garage on a cold, February morning, met it in a blast of gunfire and a bright white light that dissolved into nothingness.

And then suddenly they were back, all seven of them, walking around on the streets, staring at each other in shock. It was the day before Valentine's Day, February 13. But it was one year later: 1930.

It didn't take long for the ground rules to be made apparent. They returned to Chicago for no more than forty-eight hours, the seven of them suddenly showing up at the old garage. They couldn't hurt anyone—Drago was the first to discover that when he tried to rob a taxi driver. They simply wandered around the city for two days and then vanished back into the void once more. Until the next Valentine's Day rolled around.

It wasn't until several years had passed that they realized there was an escape from the endless cycle. One of the Scazzetti brothers fell in love with a girl from his old neighborhood. And this time when they returned Scazzetti was still there, happily married.

One by one the men had fallen, finding someone to love them, finding someone to love, living out their new lives in married bliss, until the mid-eighties, when only Billy, Drago and Rafferty were left. Rafferty had assumed no force in heaven or earth could change Drago's murderous ways, but a sweet-faced woman named Lizzie had worked miracles.

Billy followed the next year, and it wasn't until he'd gone to Mary O'Hanahan Moretti that Rafferty realized that the kid had been holding out, afraid to leave him alone with Drago. The thought amused him. He'd spent enough time around psychopaths like Drago—he was more than capable of taking care of himself. Besides, Drago was unable to hurt anyone as long as he lived in the St. Valentine's Day limbo the others did.

It had been three years since Billy had left. Three years that Rafferty returned, alone, on a frosty February morning to spend his forty-eight hours of life. The Scazzetti brothers had died in the fifties. Richstein and Von Trebbenhoff were long gone. Drago had moved with his wife to a suburb, and Billy kept his distance. True love had transformed Drago, but there was too much history to forget everything.

Rafferty viewed the entire process with hard-core cynicism. Some years he came back to disaster. The Depression had been very bad in Chicago, and even the novelty of being able to buy a drink in public hadn't offset the despairing mood of the entire city.

The war was probably the worst. Those three years had been torment, knowing people were dying for their country, knowing all they could do was float in limbo. Drago had joined up, of course, more intent on killing Krauts than being patriotic, but he'd left after forty-eight hours all the same. Only the Scazzetti brothers had managed to serve, having settled into their new lives in time.

Rafferty had hated the late forties and fifties. He'd spent his forty-eight hours for almost a decade sitting in a bar, drinking and smoking.

The sixties were insane—too crazy for him to even try to comprehend. Two days every year was not enough time for him to catch up with the changing world, and by the sixties he no longer even tried.

By the seventies he was into hedonism. It was an easy enough matter to find a willing woman and spend the forty-eight hours in bed. Which was exactly what he did. He didn't believe in love, or second chances, and nothing he saw during his brief sojourns changed his mind. Not even his friends' happiness, or the promise of life lived out to its natural conclusion, could dent his hard-core cynicism.

And now here he was in the nineties. Things had begun to move so rapidly he no longer made any attempt to catch up. He simply arrived, looked around and did his best to satisfy his physical needs, for cigarettes, for a drink, for sex and food. And then he was gone again.

Until Billy started dragging him back into feeling again. He thought he had everything taken care of. Billy had his own comfortable life, the others were long gone. He could spend his two days in a single-minded pursuit of pleasure, with no one's needs to interfere, to make him start thinking.

But the years had changed him. Decades ago he could have turned his back on Billy and his wife. Decades ago he could have ignored the danger Ricky Drago posed to innocent people. After all, he'd worked side by side with the man in the twenties, he'd watched with distant horror the kind of bloodbath Drago could instigate.

He'd changed, and it made him angry. He'd already blown a good four hours on Billy's problems and a woman who wasn't the type to put out, and he didn't relish wasting any more time trying to save the world from the likes of Ricky Drago. That was Ms. Emerson's province. Let her provide the sainthood. As for him, he needed a drink.

It took less than two hours to get Billy Moretti released, the charges dropped. In retrospect, Rafferty wondered why the hell he'd bothered with organized crime when being a lawyer seemed so much sleazier. He watched with awe and respect as Helen Emerson went from one superior to the next, sweet-talking one, arguing with another, being humble and deferential with the third while she managed to convince the man that letting Billy Moretti off this time was his idea in the first place.

"You're going to be on tighter probation," she told Billy as she waited by the elevator. "It's the best I can do for you."

Billy was still looking uncomfortably pale. "I appreciate it." He cast a beseeching glance at Rafferty.

"The next time you won't be so lucky," Rafferty said in his most lawyerly voice as the elevator door opened. "I'll keep an eye on him, Ms. Emerson."

She just looked at him. Funny, how people thought glasses ruined a woman's looks. He was starting to like hers. Maybe it was because she had such terrific warm brown eyes in the first place. "See that you do, Mr. Rafferty. Or the next time he won't be so lucky."

"There won't be a next time," Billy said. Rafferty thought of Ricky Drago, and wondered.

They stepped into the creaky old elevator, and Rafferty shoved his hands into his pockets. He'd wanted to touch her, to shake hands with her, hell, to kiss her goodbye. He wasn't going to see her again, and for the first time in his endless, misspent time on earth he found he regretted that. He leaned back against the elevator, giving her a wry smile. "See you," he said, having mastered that bit of jargon from the seventies, even knowing he wasn't going to see her at all.

She didn't want him to go. He knew that, as well as if she'd telegraphed it. "Thanks for the breakfast," she called, just before the doors slid shut.

"You bought Ms. Emerson breakfast?" Billy muttered in disbelief. "I can't believe it."

"Can't believe I can be a gentleman?" Rafferty countered. "I buy women breakfast all the time."

"Yeah, but they usually earn it the night before."

"What makes you think Ms. Emerson didn't?" Even saying it, he felt faintly rotten. Helen Emerson wasn't the kind of woman you ruffled the sheets with and then paid off with a fancy breakfast. He knew that the moment he saw her—it had been one of his reasons for feeling so uneasy.

"She's not that kind of woman," Billy was saying.

"Billy, Billy," he chided. "Every woman is that kind of woman. Once they meet the right man."

"Are you the right man for Ms. Emerson?"

"Me? Forget it. I've told you a million times before, true love and all that garbage isn't for Mrs. Rafferty's son Jamey. I like my life just fine. Forty-eight hours a year with no bills, no regrets, no responsibilities. It suits me fine."

"Sure, Rafferty," Billy said, his voice disbelieving. "So what are we going to do about Drago?"

They'd stepped out into the chill February air. The day had brightened, marginally, but the wind was still whipping through the streets, and Rafferty shivered, pulling his old overcoat around him more tightly.

"What do you mean, what are we going to do about Drago? He'll keep away from you from now on—that's one thing you can thank Ms. Emerson for. Now that you've been picked up in connection with the Carnahan robbery, Drago would be a sitting duck if he's seen with you. He might be crazy but he was never stupid. He'll lie low, find someone else to terrorize."

"That's the problem. It's not just Mary and me I'm worried about," Billy said earnestly.

"You worry about the fate of the world, Billy," he said, lighting another cigarette, cupping his hands to shield the flame from the brisk north wind. "After all these years, haven't you learned there's not a damned thing you can do about it?"

"I wouldn't be here if I believed that."

Rafferty shrugged, shaking out the match and tossing it onto the sidewalk. "You can't stop Drago, Billy."

"I can't just stand by and let him do it, either."

"Do what?"

"I told you, he's crazy. When his wife was killed he sort of went off the deep end."

Rafferty sighed. He didn't want to hear this, didn't want to get involved, but Billy had always been impossibly stubborn. "How was she killed?"

"In a car accident. Drago was driving."

Rafferty swore. "That's tough."

"Tough enough. I figure Drago had two choices. To blame himself, or to blame someone else."

"I can guess what Drago chose. Who's he blaming? Was there another driver involved?"

"Nope. Drago was driving recklessly, and the car skidded into a cement bridge. He was furious because he'd been brought in for questioning."

He knew what was coming. He'd never been psychic in his life, but by now he knew the kinds of tricks fate played on him. "And?"

"And he blames the prosecutor who brought him in. He told me he was going to kill her, that it's just a matter of time and circumstance. I believe him, Rafferty. He'll do it."

"I don't have to ask who the prosecutor was, do I?" He took a deep drag on the cigarette. It no longer tasted as wonderful. It was no surprise—sixty-four-year-old cigarettes lose something of their punch.

"Ms. Emerson."

"Does she know?"

"I don't think so," Billy said. "It's been a couple of years. Drago's been biding his time. But she's put a spoke in his wheels this time around, and she's got enough on him to go after him, even if I don't cooperate. He's got nothing else to lose. He'd go after her this time, and a man like Drago doesn't miss."

"Hell and damnation," Rafferty said again. "So what do you want from me, Billy? You think I can confront Drago, talk some sense into him? He doesn't have any sense."

Billy shook his head. "He's off the deep end, I told you. I don't know what you can do about it, what either of us can do about it, short of going to Ms.

Emerson and trying to explain. Problem is, I'd have to explain what I was doing hanging around with someone like Drago, and you know I'm a lousy liar."

"You always were." He refused to sound sympathetic. He didn't want to get trapped in this situation. Trapped with saving Helen Emerson.

"I have to get back to Mary. She's probably been worried sick about me, and this pregnancy hasn't been easy on her. I just need to spend some time with her, the next day or two. When you have to ...uh...leave, then I can take over. Maybe in the meantime we could come up with a believable story to warn her."

Rafferty stared at him for a long moment before dropping the cigarette onto the sidewalk and crushing it beneath his shoe. "No."

"Come on, Rafferty, it's only a couple of days...."

"It's my *only* couple of days. I'm not going to spend it baby-sitting for an uptight virgin."

"Rafferty..."

"No!" he said, raising his voice. "I can't help you. You know as well as I do that there's nothing I could do to stop Drago anyway, as long as I'm here on borrowed time. Go check on Mary, then make an anonymous phone call or something to warn the woman. Drago's already waited this long—he'll wait another day or two."

"I don't think so," Billy said.

"It's not my problem. I stick my neck out for nobody, you know that. I've already wasted too much time dealing with your problems, and I'm late for a very heavy date with a certain lady."

"What lady?"

"I don't know—I haven't met her yet. But she'll be stacked, blond and willing. And with any luck I won't have to set foot out of a hotel room for the next thirty-six hours." He glanced at his wristwatch and swore. "Damn it, I've already wasted half the day!"

Billy just looked at him. Rafferty was used to that expression; he'd seen it on his mother's face often enough when he was growing up. He'd disappointed Billy. The hell with it. He was sick and tired of being a good guy. He wasn't going to feel guilty.

"Hell and damnation," he said aloud. "You aren't going to do this to me, Billy. I don't care." And he stalked off down the sidewalk, the icy Chicago wind whipping through his hair, his coat collar pulled up high.

He got no more than three blocks. Three blocks to think about Billy's expression, like that of a beaten dog. Three blocks to think of Mary Moretti, her belly swollen with a troublesome pregnancy, lost and frightened and needing her husband. Three blocks to think about Ms. Emerson, with her huge eyes and untidy apartment, with her kissable mouth and wonderful legs. And her innocence—he couldn't forget that. Not to mention a family full of cops. Couldn't her brothers and father protect her?

A light snow had begun to fall when he wheeled around and started back, cursing beneath his breath. He didn't even know how he was going to convince Helen Emerson that she should accept his company. She hadn't been any too sure of him in the first place, and he couldn't up and tell her she was the target of a madman.

He'd worry about that when the question came up. He'd always been adept at convincing women he was attracted to them, and with the bespectacled, be-suited, untidy Ms. Emerson it wasn't going to be that much of a stretch, illogical as it was. He *was* attracted to her—that was half his problem.

She was just coming down the broad front steps when he saw her. She was wearing that ridiculous puffy coat, and she was clutching a pile of folders against her chest. The wind was tossing her long hair into her eyes, and she shoved it out of the way as she stepped onto the sidewalk.

He stood watching, wondering how he was going to explain his sudden return, when he heard the sound of the car. A sound he'd heard too many times, too many years ago, the throaty rev of a car about to speed through a crowded city, intent on disaster. He turned, in time to see the anonymous black sedan come hur-tling around the corner.

Heading straight for Helen Emerson.

Chapter Three

For a moment Rafferty couldn't move, rooted to his spot on the sidewalk as he watched disaster about to unfold. He'd been a witness too many times, stood silent and unmoving as the grisly violence of gangland Chicago tactics took their toll. He'd met his own fate that way, at the end of a machine gun. He couldn't stand by and let it happen again.

He moved then, fast, barreling into Ms. Emerson full force, knocking both of them onto the sidewalk in a tangle of limbs and folders. In the distance he could hear the screech of tires as the car backed up and sped away, and he closed his eyes in a brief, silent moment of thankfulness.

"Would you like to get off me?" Helen Emerson said in a voice that was both tart and breathless.

He opened his eyes and looked down into hers. Her glasses had been knocked off, and her face was pale with shock. Her breathing was rapid, her heartbeat racing against his, and he figured he better get off her damned quick before she figured he was hard.

Of course, Ms. Emerson struck him as such an innocent that she might not even recognize his condition. He climbed off her, standing up and reaching down to haul her up beside him. For a moment she didn't touch him, and her expression was both dazed and hostile, before she finally put her smaller, fine-boned hand in his and let him pull her to her feet.

"Why'd you do that?" Her voice sounded dazed, rusty.

"I thought you were going to be hit by a car."

Her face turned even paler, and she swayed slightly. "You mean someone was trying to kill me?" she squeaked out.

He caught her arms with his hands, resisting the impulse to pull her against him, to warm her with his warmth, shield her with his strength. He held her loosely, ready to tighten his grip if she should sway again. "Of course not," he said easily, convincingly. "I just saw someone take the corner too damned fast and I decided I'd better make my move. He didn't come anywhere near you, but I couldn't be sure of that ahead of time. He must have been drunk."

As a matter of fact the driver of the car had come so damned close Rafferty had felt the tail of his coat whip against the hood of the car, but Helen was too shook-up to realize the truth.

"You didn't get a license plate number, did you?" She stepped back pushing a hand through her long dark hair. Her hand was trembling.

"Too many numbers," he said, shaking his head. In his day things had been a lot easier, and memorizing a license plate didn't take a Ph.D. Of course, knowing the number wouldn't do any good. Ricky Drago would have used a stolen car for his murderous little excursion.

"You were very fast," she said. "You may have saved my life. I . . . thank you."

She didn't want to be beholden, he could see that. And while part of him wanted to lie and say she'd been perfectly safe, he still needed to stick to her like glue. Something had clicked in, made the decision for him. This was going to be one two-day sojourn where he did his saint impersonation. He was going to look out for Helen Emerson and keep Ricky Drago at a safe distance. By February 15 it would be someone else's responsibility.

"No problem," he said, liking that particular phrase. "I was known as Fast Jamey when I played college football."

"Where did you go?"

As a matter of fact, he'd been one of the few members of the Chicago underworld to have graduated from an Ivy League school. Harvard had never been particularly proud of this particular alumnus, but Bugs Moran had found it amusing to order him around. "Harvard," he said.

"You don't look very Ivy League," she said, moving away from him.

"Yeah, I know. And I don't look like a lawyer. Exactly what do I look like, Ms. Emerson?" His voice was cool and mocking.

"Humphrey Bogart."

"I beg your pardon?" She'd managed to throw him a curve. There was a trace of color back in her pale cheeks, and her dark eyes were beginning to sparkle.

"Crossed with a little bit of John Garfield in his prime. And maybe just a touch of Cary Grant when he was being evil."

"You telling me I look like a movie star?" he demanded.

She shook her head. "No, Mr. Rafferty. I'm telling you you look like a gangster."

IT DIDN'T MAKE the slightest bit of sense to her, and Helen Emerson had always prided herself on being sensible, at least in her dealings with the opposite sex. There was no reason in the world for her to be sitting in a crowded luncheonette, across from someone who looked like a time-traveling gangster, albeit a dangerously, seductively appealing one, and watch while he devoured more cholesterol than she ate in a month, smoked cigarettes and coddled her.

She did feel coddled, though, and that was probably the reason she was there. He'd whisked her away from the busy sidewalk, taken her into Murphy's Diner and plied her with tea and a little tin of aspirin that looked as if it had to be half a century old. He'd picked up her scattered papers, wrapped her coat tightly around her, put his hand under her arm and steered her to a small haven of quiet and safety, ignoring her weak protests that she could manage on her own. Of course she could. She just wasn't sure she wanted to.

He was trying to charm her. She knew that perfectly well—she hadn't been a prosecutor for three years without being able to recognize when a defense lawyer was trying to flatter her. Of course, Rafferty had no reason. She'd already let Billy Moretti walk, and even if she felt a twinge of guilt about that, her instincts still insisted she'd been right.

Her instincts also told her that James Rafferty wouldn't hurt her. Even if he kept his gaze shuttered and his charm surface, she knew deep inside that he was no threat to her. Except to her peace of mind.

Maybe she was a fool to listen to her instincts. They weren't infallible, even if they'd served her well for most of her life. If she had any of the common sense her family believed her to have she'd dismiss Rafferty and the odd, trembling effect he was having on her senses, and get on with her life.

But she wasn't going to do that. She'd already told her boss she was taking the rest of the day off—going back would look more than odd. And while she ought to get rid of Rafferty, she couldn't bring herself to do it. He'd leave her soon enough, once he was certain she'd gotten over her scare.

Funny, she hadn't seen any car heading her way. She still wasn't quite certain if she believed him—after all, cars didn't just mow people down as a matter of course. But if there'd been no car, what was it he wanted from her? And would she be willing to give it to him?

He leaned back and lit a cigarette without asking, taking in a deep drag of the unfiltered tobacco. "Don't you know how bad those things are for you?" she asked in a disapproving voice.

"I expect you'll tell me," he replied, blowing a lazy smoke ring in her direction. She watched, fascinated, as it drifted and floated across the table, dissipating in front of her eyes like a fairy garland.

Absurd thought, when it was toxic waste dancing in her direction. "It'll kill you," she said flatly.

He smiled then, a wry, self-mocking smile that was as appealing as it was irritating. "No, it won't."

"The surgeon general . . ."

"The surgeon general doesn't know squat," Rafferty said, leaning back and watching her from behind hooded eyes. "I'm not going to die from lung cancer."

"Emphysema, then."

"Not that, either. I'll probably go out in a hail of bullets, like something out of *Scarface.*"

"You've been seeing too many movies."

"So have you," he replied. "As a matter of fact, I prefer old movies. Very old movies. But then, I'm older than you are."

"Not by much."

"You'd be surprised," he murmured, stubbing out the cigarette. "Are you ready to go?"

"Go where?"

"I'm driving you home."

"I'm perfectly capable of driving myself," she said.

"No, you're not. Even when you're feeling fine you're a lousy driver. You're too slow and cautious. I was amazed we made it downtown in one piece. After a shake-up like you just had you'd probably plow into an ice truck before you made it halfway home."

"An ice truck?" Helen was mystified.

Rafferty didn't even blink. "Don't they deliver ice in Chicago? To bars and hotels and such."

"I suppose so, but . . ."

"Don't argue with me, Helen. I'm driving you home and that's that."

She stared up at him. "I don't like being told what to do," she said sharply. "I grew up with four brothers and a father who all thought they knew what was best for me, and if I were the slightest bit of a wimp they would have walked all over me. I make my own decisions in this life."

"What kind of decisions did they try to make for you?" he asked, draining his cup of coffee.

"They didn't want me to go to law school. They didn't want me to work for the State's Attorney. They wanted me to marry a boy I grew up with and have babies and be a good cop's wife."

"And you didn't want to."

"No," she said flatly. "I don't think I'll ever get married."

"Come on, counselor, you're a little long in the tooth but you're not that bad-looking," he murmured.

She stared at him in shock, before she realized he was teasing her. "It's kind of you to say so," she replied in a dulcet tone. "As a matter of fact, I haven't yet met anyone who's worthy of me." She leaned back, surveying him with a cool air, and for the first time she realized what a benefit a cigarette could be. She would have loved to take a deep drag and blow a cool stream of smoke directly into those challenging dark eyes.

He just looked at her for a moment, and a smile curved his mouth. It was different from his other smiles—there was no trace of mockery this time, and his dark, brooding eyes lightened for a moment. "Too bad, Ms. Emerson. Maybe you'll just have to die a virgin."

She knocked over her tea. Fortunately she'd finished most of it, and the puddle of dark liquid spread across the table at a slow enough rate to keep her busy mopping it up with paper napkins, hoping he wouldn't notice the dark flush that had risen to her face. How in God's name did he know? Did he have X-ray vision or something?

He rose, tossing a handful of bills down on the table. "Come on, counselor. You're still a bit unsteady."

She glared at him, but it did no good. He just continued to look at her out of those steady, amused eyes, and if she pushed it he'd probably say something even more outrageous. "You can drive me home," she allowed. "But only because I'm not interested in arguing with you."

"What are you interested in doing with me, Helen?"

"Getting rid of you as fast as I can. I'm assuming the best way to do that is to let you drive me home."

"You're a fast learner," he said. "Give me your keys."

"Come on, now, Rafferty," she complained, loath to give in.

He just stood in front of her, hand outstretched. "The keys."

She looked down at his hand. It was a surprisingly elegant hand, with long, deft fingers, a narrow palm, a strong wrist with a thin, old-fashioned gold watch. "Bully," she said, reaching into her jumbled purse for the keys.

He held the passenger door for her when they reached the car, a first-time occurrence for Helen that she viewed with mistrust. She wasn't used to men holding doors for her, putting their strong, hard hands under her elbow, taking care of her. She didn't like it. Even if she found it dangerously seductive.

He probably only opened the door to keep her from jumping into the driver's seat, she thought grumpily as she fastened her seat belt around her. She watched with covert interest as he climbed in beside her, folding his long legs into her compact car with all the elegant disdain of a circus clown climbing into a miniature car with twelve of his cohorts and a chimpanzee besides. He stared at the regulation dashboard for a long, intent moment, as if it were something comparable to the space shuttle, and he made no effort to fasten his seat belt.

"You *do* know how to drive, don't you?" Helen asked.

"I'm used to a bigger car." He turned the key until the starter whined in pain, then stared down at the floor. "Where's the clutch?"

"I don't need one. This is an automatic. Are you sure you know how to drive?"

"Yes." He still made no move to put the car into Drive.

"You know what an automatic is, don't you? You just push the little knob to D for Drive and then you aim the car. Very simple."

"Very simple," he muttered, pushing the gear stick. The car surged forward, he stomped on the brake and Helen banged her head on the window.

"Terrific," she muttered. "You'd better wear your seat belt. For one thing, it's the law. For another, I get the feeling we're not about to have the smoothest ride."

For some reason the seat belt seemed just as foreign to him as the automatic transmission. He was cursing under his breath, polite enough curses, as he dealt with the thing, then he turned his attention to the traffic. "You usually drive through this stuff?" he asked in horror. "How in the hell did they manage to make so many cars?"

"There are lots of people in Chicago, Rafferty, and all of them drive."

"The hell with it," he said. And pulled out directly in front of a very large pickup truck.

He might not drive well, but he drove very fast. They missed the pickup, avoided a Mercedes, scraped the highway divider and skidded past a taxi. He was hunched over the small steering wheel of her car, and he seemed out of place, out of time in her tiny little car.

"You're not used to foreign cars, are you?" she asked, clutching the door handle and surreptitiously pressing her own feet to the floor every time she wished he would brake.

"No." He yanked the steering wheel, whipping around the corner and heading back toward Elm Street. He might not know much about her car but his sense of direction was impeccable. He was using shortcuts it had taken her months to find.

"What was your first car?" She tried steady breathing to calm herself as he zipped in between two huge delivery trucks.

"An old Packard," he muttered, reaching into his pocket for his cigarettes.

"No!" she shrieked. In a calmer voice she managed to say, "I'd rather you didn't smoke."

"Don't tell me. This is a smoke-free car," he said wryly, taking a corner on two tires.

"Not particularly. I'd just prefer you to keep both hands on the wheel."

"You could always light it for me."

For a moment she was struck dumb. She hated cigarettes; they were nasty, smelly things. She hated smokers with their noxious cloud and their disregard for other people's lungs. And yet the thought of lighting a cigarette for James Rafferty, moving it from her mouth to his, was almost unbearably erotic.

"No cigarettes," she said flatly.

"I expected as much."

"I've never even seen a Packard. Weren't they luxury cars from the thirties?"

"They had 'em in the twenties and the forties, too. I had one of the last models."

"I bet it was wonderful."

"It was big. And fast." He zoomed through an intersection just as the light turned red, missing a pedestrian by mere inches.

"Do you think you could drive a little slower?" she asked through gritted teeth.

"No. I need a cigarette."

"Do you know how bad those things are for you?"

"Do you know how much smokers hate to hear about how bad those things are for you?"

"Slow down and I won't lecture."

"Let me smoke and I'll slow down."

Stalemate. The rest of the drive was in a silence punctuated only by the squeal of brakes and the muffled shrieks of terror. She finally gave up and closed her eyes, gripping the seat with both hands and offering a hopeful prayer to the paternalistic Catholic God of her childhood. When she opened her eyes the car had pulled to a stop, directly outside her tumbledown building.

"How do I stop this thing?" he grumbled, already reaching for his cigarettes.

"P for Park. Just think mnemonics." Her hands were shaking slightly as she unfastened her seat belt. All in all, her day had been too damned exciting, and it was barely past noon.

"Just think what?" He'd turned off the car, fumbled clumsily with his own seat belt before climbing out onto the sidewalk.

"Never mind." She opened her door before he could do it for her, and he had to content himself with smoking his damned cigarette. She held out her hand, knowing she needed to get rid of him. Knowing that she didn't want to. "I really appreciate everything you've done."

He looked down at her, and there was a faint trace of amusement in his dark, cynical eyes. "Are you trying to give me the brush-off?"

An odd turn of phrase. "Of course not," she stammered.

"Good," he said. "Because I'd love to come in for a cup of coffee."

"I think I'm out of coffee."

"I'll drink water."

"Chicago water?" she echoed. "You've got to be kidding."

"You mean you can't even drink the water anymore?" he demanded, astonished. "What the hell happened to this city? You can't smoke, you can't drive though the millions of cars on the road and now you're telling me you can't even drink the goddamned water? I can't say I think much about progress. People were better off in the twenties."

"How would you know?"

That stopped him. He shrugged, and once more there was that charming, false smile on his face. "Just a guess." He didn't touch her, but then, he didn't have to. Even standing almost a foot away, his presence was a tangible thing, intense and overpowering. It didn't make sense, the attraction that was stronger than anything she'd ever felt in her life. She couldn't be that drawn to a distant, mocking stranger.

But she was.

"I probably have some instant."

For a moment he looked blank. "Instant?" he echoed.

"Instant coffee. You said you wanted coffee, remember? I think I used up the last of my beans, but I might still have an old jar left over. If you're not fussy."

He just looked at her for a moment. An endless, eternal moment, and she had the strange feeling she'd made a much greater commitment than sharing a simple cup of coffee. That somehow she'd offered him much much more than that.

"I'm not fussy," he said in his deep voice. And as he followed her up the short flight of steps to her front door, she wondered whether she might have made a very big mistake.

And she knew she didn't care.

She was messy, all right, Rafferty thought as he surveyed the living room with its three layers of peeling wallpaper, its piles of newspapers, the breakfast and dinner dishes and files and clothing littering the table. His mother had always kept a spotlessly neat house. It had been her pride and joy and his constant frustration. A man could feel at home in a place like this.

On top of the untidy comfort of the place, there was one of the largest televisions he'd ever seen. He had no doubt it was color, and while he couldn't begin to guess what the oblong black boxes on top of it were, they probably had something to do with it.

He was a man who loved television. Anything from a black-and-white ten-inch screen to one of the huge color models like Helen favored, and he loved everything that was on. Baseball games, hockey games, football games. Beer commercials and soap operas and game shows. The first year he discovered television in the hotel room he'd shared with a willing young lady from Evanston he'd spent the entire time in front of it, ignoring the siren call of a gorgeous woman. He'd learned to moderate his time in successive visits, but the sight of that huge television put lust in his heart as nothing else had.

"I know, I know," Helen said, coming in with a steaming mug of coffee in an astonishingly short time. "The television's obscene."

"Is it?" He glanced over at it with great curiosity. He'd seen one of those channels in the hotel, surprised and amused to see that certain things hadn't changed at all in the last fifty years.

"I mean the size of it. Not to mention a cable box and two VCRs. I happen to like TV."

"So do I."

She wasn't mollified. Apparently liking television was considered shameful nowadays. He couldn't imagine why anyone would disapprove of such a wonder.

"I only watch PBS," she said defensively.

"Sure," he said, mystified.

"And old movies. Musicals, gangster movies, all that kind of stuff. Black-and-white classics."

"You prefer black-and-white?" he asked, astonished. Color movies had been a wonder to him; he couldn't understand how anyone could prefer shades of gray.

She shrugged. "What can I say? I'm a throwback."

He almost spilled his coffee. "Are you?" he asked very carefully.

She managed a self-deprecating smile. "My father says I was born in the wrong decade. I would have been better off in the thirties or forties."

"What about the twenties?" His voice sounded harsh even to his ears.

She didn't notice. "Not the twenties," she said flatly. "Chicago was too violent."

He didn't like this conversation. Didn't like the implications of her innocent statement. "It probably was," he said. He decided to change the subject. "How did you make the coffee that fast?"

"I have a microwave."

Somehow he'd missed that during his previous sojourns. It sounded like something out of Buck Rogers, and tasted like liquid cardboard. Another thing that hadn't improved in more than half a century. "Very nice," he said.

"You're a liar, Mr. Rafferty."

He didn't flinch. "Just Rafferty," he said. "And why do you say that?"

"For one thing, that coffee is at least two years old, the crystals were a solid mass that I had to scrape from the bottom of the jar and it wasn't very good to begin."

He gave her a cool smile. "It's not such a terrible lie, is it? My mother raised me to be polite."

"I'm sure she did. I just wonder about your other lies."

"Other lies?"

"I don't think you're who you say you are, Rafferty. And I trust my instincts." She took a sip of the coffee, then made a face. She looked very calm, very self-controlled, but he could see the ripple of tension beneath the surface. "You want to tell me the truth?"

He considered it, for one crazy moment, just for the pleasure of seeing her shock. He'd never tried the truth on a woman, and he wasn't about to start now. He leaned back, pulled out his cigarettes and smiled blandly. "You'll never believe it, sugar."

"Try me."

He glanced at her over the flame of the wooden match, his eyes meeting hers for a heated moment. And then she blushed, the kind of shy, innocent blush he hadn't seen for decades. "Who are you, Rafferty?" she said. "And what do you want from me?"

Chapter Four

Helen didn't trust him. There were any number of reasons for her not to, including the basic fact that when Abramowitz called her to ask about Billy Moretti he'd insisted he had no one named Rafferty working for him.

She'd accepted that information with a sick feeling of doom. She didn't usually make mistakes like that, mistakes of trust. She'd thought Billy Moretti was worth another chance. She thought James Rafferty was one of the good guys. Instead he turned out to be a liar.

It still couldn't shake the basic fact that she trusted him. Maybe not to tell her the truth, but to do the right thing.

She hadn't seen the car he said was about to run her down—for all she knew he might have made that up, too. But none of it made sense. He had what he wanted—Billy Moretti was walking around free, she'd dropped the charges and there was no way she could bring them up again, not and keep her credibility.

So why, when she'd gotten the feeling he was walking out of her life, had he returned to literally sweep her off her feet? Why had he taken her to that coffee shop and plied her with tea and toast, why had he driven her home, why was he sitting in her apartment drinking the worst coffee known to man and watching her out of wary eyes, obviously deciding which lie to try next?

And what was even more troubling to her was why had she let him?

Instincts, again. Those irrational, damnable things that had gotten her into more trouble in her life, her instincts were telling her to trust this man. Not his words, which were mostly a bunch of flattery, blather and outright lies. But to trust *him*.

And despite what her common sense told her, she did.

"What do you mean, who am I?" he said, stalling for time, fiddling with his cigarette. "I told you . . ."

"You told me a pack of lies. Abramowitz has never heard of you."

He didn't look the slightest bit abashed. "Maybe he's got a short memory."

"Abramowitz has a mind like a steel trap. You lied to me, Rafferty. You aren't a lawyer."

"I had a year of law school," he said, and she was so bemused by his nonchalance that she didn't tell him to put out the cigarette.

"What law school?"

"Princeton."

"Princeton doesn't have a law school."

Rafferty shrugged. "Actually it was prelaw, and it was at Harvard."

"You don't look like a Harvard man."

He had the gall to smile at her, his dark eyes crinkling. "If you aren't going to believe me, why bother asking?" He leaned back against her shabby, overstuffed sofa, stretching his long legs out in front of him.

She stood staring at him, unwilling to sit while she cross-examined him. To sit would be to accept his presence, and she wasn't ready to do that. Any more than she was ready to send him on his way. "Why did you lie to me?"

"I didn't actually lie to you. You jumped to a number of conclusions, and I went along with them. It seemed easier than trying to set you straight."

"Do you always do things the easy way?" she asked, watching him.

"I try," he said, and that aura of stillness invaded the apartment. "Sit down, Helen, and I'll answer your questions. Truthfully."

"You'll answer my questions, and then you'll leave," she said, using the cool, self-controlled voice that had managed to convince dozens of defense lawyers and any number of jurors. "And I prefer to stand."

It didn't fool Rafferty. "Sit down," he said, in a quiet, deadly voice.

Helen sat.

She almost wished she had a cup of that horrible coffee for herself. Anything to keep her busy, to occupy her while she studied him. As it was, there was nothing she could look at but him, with his dark, slightly mocking eyes and distant, handsome face. "I presume you're some friend of Billy Moretti's, and you flew in to see whether you could get him off." She couldn't stand the intensity of his eyes. His old-fashioned silk tie seemed a safer place to look.

"You're doing it again."

"Doing what?"

"Jumping to conclusions. Trust me, I didn't fly in. No wings."

"Very funny," Helen said, steeling herself to meet his gaze. "Then why don't you tell me the truth?"

"No problem," he said. "You got an ashtray?"

She hadn't even realized he'd been polluting her smoke-free apartment. "Use your saucer," she said sharply.

"Aren't you going to tell me not to smoke?"

He read her that easily. "I doubt if it would do any good," she replied.

"I don't know. If you asked real nice . . ."

"Put out the damned cigarette and don't smoke," Helen snapped.

He smiled at her, without a trace of mockery. "That's better. I like a little honesty myself." He stubbed out the cigarette, and she noticed his hands again. Long, deft fingers, beautiful hands. With no rings. "You're right, I'm an old friend of Billy's. His wife got in touch with me when he got into trouble. You knew as well as I did that he was set up—Billy

Moretti is one of nature's good guys. He didn't deserve to take a fall for a creep like Morris.''

"Is that what he told you? Did Morris force him?
Will he testify?'' she asked eagerly, forgetting her distrust, leaning closer in her chair.

"No."

"No, what?"

"No to everything. You don't understand the code,
counselor. He would have gone to Joliet, his baby
would be born without a father, his wife and child
would be on welfare or maybe even the streets before
he'd rat on a brother. How long have you been a lawyer?"

"Five years, and I understand..."

"You don't understand a damned thing. You're
from the other side, lady. I saw that picture in your
office. That family portrait of Cops, Incorporated.
We speak a different language, come from a different
world. Billy and I are a different race, a different
time...." He let it trail off, as if surprised at himself.

"You and Billy don't strike me as having that much
in common," she said.

He just looked at her from across the room. "That
goes to show how much you know."

"You must be at least ten years older than he is.
You're from an Ivy League background, I'll believe
that much, and I know Billy's rap sheet."

"We have other things in common."

She felt a little shiver slip down her spine at his deep,
implacable voice. She wasn't sure if she liked his voice
or not. There was no question that it had an astonish-

ing effect on her, turning her bones to jelly. He wasn't the kind of man she was used to. She was used to the boisterous, emotional outbursts of her rough and ready family. She was used to the gentlemanly tactics of her occasional dates. She was used to the camaraderie of the men at work. She wasn't used to whatever it was Rafferty represented.

"I just want you to explain to me..." she began, when she was interrupted by the shrill ring of her telephone. She ignored it. "...explain to me..." she continued.

"Aren't you going to get the phone?"

"I'll let the answering machine do it."

He stared at her with a blank look, as if she'd been speaking Japanese. "Answering machine?"

She might have almost thought he didn't know what an answering machine was. Impossible, of course, unless he'd just flown in from Mars. "Don't try to distract me, Rafferty, I'm on to you," she snapped.

"I doubt it."

"Just tell me..." She stopped as the machine clicked on, and a familiar voice sounded from the speaker.

"Er, Ms. Emerson, this is Billy Moretti. I...er...was just wondering..."

With a weary sigh Helen picked up the receiver. "I'm here, Billy," she said. "I expect you're looking for Rafferty. Hold on a minute."

"He's there?" There was no mistaking the shock in Billy's voice.

"He's here." She handed the phone to Rafferty. "I'll give you and your 'client' some privacy," she said, rising and heading for the bathroom. The low murmur of voices followed her.

As a matter of fact, she was the one who needed the privacy. As she closed the door of the huge, ornate bathroom behind her, shutting out the sound of conversation, she turned to look at herself in the gilded three-paneled mirror that Crystal had loved.

She barely recognized herself. It was no wonder— she'd survived a flying tackle by the deceptively strong man now lounging on her sofa. Her reddish-brown hair was a wild tangle, her face was pale and her eyes looked huge and a little shocked. She pulled off her glasses, splashed water on her skin and shook her head, trying to shake some sense back into her disordered brain. She needed to get that lying interloper out of her apartment, out of her life. It was too late to do anything about Billy Moretti, and if she'd been wrong, he'd come her way again soon enough.

The problem was, she didn't want to get rid of Rafferty. She wanted to listen to his raspy voice, watch his stillness, stare at his distant, handsome face. God, she wanted to do more than that. She wanted to touch him.

She slapped herself. The shock of it didn't do any good; she simply stared back at herself defiantly. "Get a hold of yourself, Emerson," she muttered, dragging a brush through her tangled hair. "You're a professional." She started to pin her hair back in a tidy little bun, but her hands were uncharacteristically clumsy. She gave up, shaking it free, hoping her glasses would restore her equilibrium. She really only needed them for reading, but she used them at other times in the vain hope they'd give her an air of cool authority. They didn't.

She had a whole box of makeup beside the sink, makeup she seldom bothered to use. She glanced up at her reflection. It must be the aftereffects of the near accident, she told herself. She needed a touch of rouge to counteract the paleness of her skin. She needed mascara to make her eyes seem less lost. She needed lipstick to give her face color.

She couldn't quite come up with an excuse for the perfume, and she stopped trying, opening the door to the bathroom and hearing nothing but silence from the living room.

Maybe he'd left. Maybe she'd never see him again. It would be the best thing possible, but she couldn't control the knot of dread curling in the bottom of her stomach as she made herself move into the living room.

Any more than she could control her brilliant smile when she saw him, still stretched out on her sofa, staring at the television with complete fascination.

"It's even more interesting when you turn it on," she said.

He glanced up at her, about to speak, when his gaze narrowed, and that aura of stillness increased, augmented by the silence. "Very nice," he said, looking at her face.

She hadn't needed the blusher. Her own natural color rose when she realized how transparent she was. She knew she ought to ignore his comment, but she couldn't. "I looked like a ghost," she said in an off-hand explanation.

There was a wry tinge to his smile. "Not like any I've been acquainted with." Before she could reply he rose, walking across the room to her, and she noticed as she had before the peculiar, stalking grace of him. "We've been invited to dinner. I accepted for both of us."

She stared up at him in numb surprise. "Excuse me?"

"You're excused. What did you do?"

"I didn't do anything. What I meant was . . ."

"What you meant, Helen," Rafferty said easily, "was how dare I accept a dinner invitation for you, when I'm allegedly here under false pretenses, I've lied to you and you probably wish I was in Hades right now."

"Hades?" For a moment she was confused.

"Hell."

"Don't swear."

"I was giving you a geographical location, not a curse. Billy wants us to come for a spaghetti dinner tonight. I told him we would. I figured you'd want to see for yourself that you made the right decision in letting him go. See how rehabilitated he is. Am I right?"

He was giving her the perfect excuse, and he knew it. He probably knew she didn't want him to leave, to disappear from her life. He was a man who knew far too much about women, and what kind of effect he had on them. But he didn't know what kind of woman she was, that she wasn't comfortable with casual relationships and friendly sex.

Or did he? "You're right," she said.

"Then you'll go with me?"

"What time do you want to pick me up?"

His eyes crinkled in amusement. "You mean you're willing to trust my driving again?"

"I survived once—I imagine I can survive anything."

"The fact of the matter is, Helen, that I don't have a car. We might as well use yours."

"Then I'll pick *you* up. Where are you staying?" He was standing too close to her. Not that his nearness was threatening, or impolite. It was just...disturbing.

He didn't look the slightest bit abashed. "That's another problem. I haven't gotten a hotel yet. I just got in to town when I heard about Billy and I've been too busy dealing with him." He glanced at his watch, and Helen noticed absently that it was a beautiful antique—the kind her Irish grandfather had owned. "It's early afternoon now, and Billy and Mary want us by six. Why don't I just spend the afternoon here?"

Was she that pitifully obvious? She wanted him to stay, God, she wanted him to stay forever. As one final sop to her pride she tried to drag up excuses. "I have work to do," she said. "I brought home files..."

"I won't interfere. I'll just sit and watch TV."

"There's nothing on but soap operas."

"I love soap operas."

"I need to take a nap." The moment the words were out of her mouth she wished she could call them back.

There was an unmistakable gleam in his eye, but he wisely said nothing, merely smiled faintly.

"I'll keep the sound turned down."

She was crazy to fight it. She'd decided to trust him, this man who'd lied to her, who'd come to her under false pretenses, whose best friend was a convicted felon. And her common sense wasn't making a dent in that level of trust. She wanted him there, even if it was dangerously foolish on her part.

"All right," she said, unable to fight it any longer. "You can use the VCR if you'd rather watch movies."

"You'll have to show me how. I've never used one."

"Rafferty, there is no human being in the city of Chicago who can't use a VCR," she said, certain he was kidding. He just stood there, looking at her, and she found she believed him.

"All right, all right," she said, moving past him, skirting him carefully, not wanting to touch him. Simply because she wanted to touch him. "What do you want to see? I've got slapstick comedy, screwball comedy, gangster movies, lots of Alfred Hitchcock, musicals, you name it."

"Anything but gangster movies."

She smiled wryly. "Now I would have thought that would be just up your alley."

"I'm not in the mood. Give me something to make me laugh."

"How about the Marx Brothers?"

"Did they end up being in the movies?"

"Don't be ridiculous, Rafferty," she said, finding *Duck Soup* and pushing it into the VCR.

"Aren't you going to watch it with me?" he asked, as she started past him.

She wanted to go back and hide in the bathroom, wash the makeup off her face. She wanted to hole up in her bedroom, concentrating on her files and not on the six feet plus of disturbing male flesh that had somehow invaded her life.

"Of course," she said, taking the armchair that was well away from the far more comfortable sofa.

His smile was faintly knowing as he returned to the couch, stretching out on it. "Hey, Helen," he said softly as the credits flickered on the huge television set.

"What?" she said, concentrating fiercely on a movie she'd seen no less than thirty-seven times.

"I like your perfume."

MS. HELEN EMERSON was too damned easy, Rafferty thought. It made him feel guilty, a completely ridiculous emotion, given that his lies and subterfuge were to protect her, at no little cost to his own plans for forty-eight hours of pleasure.

But if she accepted him as easily, as innocently, as quickly as she had, even knowing he'd lied to her about Abramowitz and God knows what else, what possible match could she be for a psychopathic manipulator like Ricky Drago?

He no longer regretted his decision. Sure, he regretted the loss of some anonymous woman's clever body wrapped around his. But when he tried to summon up the image, all he could see was Helen's pale face and huge, brown eyes.

Not that he was going to have her wrapped around him. Or look down to see her face, her hair spread out against a white pillow, her eyes glazed and her mouth...

He shifted on the sofa. She was watching the Marx Brothers as if they were the sermon on the mount, but she wasn't laughing. Neither was he.

Why couldn't Helen Emerson be someone a little looser, a little more casual, a little more getatable? Why couldn't he simply seduce her and spend the rest of his forty-eight hours in her bed, keeping her safe? It seemed to be the most sensible solution, and with anyone else he'd at least try it, before moving on to other things.

But he wasn't going to try it with Ms. Emerson. It would be a waste of time. She might be attracted to him, and he knew women well enough to recognize that she was, but she was also a virgin, or damned close to one. She wasn't ready to go to bed with a stranger. She wasn't ready to go to bed with anyone at all.

And when she was, it wouldn't be any of his business. He'd be off in some sort of limbo, while some other man was stripping off those glasses, threading his fingers through her thick, silky hair and tilting her face back to kiss....

"Don't you like the couch?" Her cool voice startled him as he shifted once more.

"Why do you ask?"

"You keep thrashing around on it. I've always found it very comfortable."

"Then why aren't you sitting here? It's a big couch."

She shook her head with a small smile, not rising to the challenge, and his opinion of her intelligence, already high, increased. "I don't think that would be a very wise idea, Rafferty. It's not that big."

"Big enough." If he could get her to sit next to him maybe the next step would be that much easier. Hell, he should have asked for something a little more erotic than Groucho Marx and Margaret Dumont. Maybe she had something hot and steamy among those black boxes she called videos. Not that he needed any stimulation—just smelling that damned, faint perfume she'd put on was trigger enough. And he had to be going out of his head, to be having erotic fantasies about a woman who was everything foreign to a man like him. A state prosecutor, a virgin, a woman too damned near thirty and from a family of cops besides. Hell, the fact that they were from different time periods was almost a minor issue.

He liked blondes, he reminded himself. Women who knew how to have a good time without expecting anything but pleasure. He liked women who were stacked, women who giggled, women who drank and smoked and didn't mind bending a law or two here and there. Not a virgin pledged to uphold it.

So why was he practically shaking with the ache to touch her? Why did he want her more than he could remember wanting anyone in his life, including the late great Crystal Latour?

It was a short movie. She picked up another, smaller black box and pointed it toward the television, the movie flicked off, and the screen was filled with a noisy ad for underarm protection, whatever the hell that was. Why did people need to protect their armpits?

"You really like soap operas?" she asked.

"I like everything on TV," he replied, trying to keep from staring at the black piece of plastic in her hand.

"This one is supposed to be good." She tossed the little box to him, and he caught it, staring at the little buttons in fascination. A moment later the show came back on. And he couldn't have asked for anything better.

As far as he could tell, neither of the people on TV had a stitch of clothing on. The long-haired man was lying on top of the woman, a sheet pulled discreetly over his hips, and he was kissing her with an enthusiasm Rafferty found commendable, if a little unnecessary at that stage of the game. They were both moaning, and the music in the background was fairly torrid as well.

"You want to change the channel, Rafferty?" Helen said in a strangled voice.

He turned to look at her, keeping his gaze innocent. "Why?"

She was blushing again, and he wondered how anyone could be so innocent in a world that had grown astonishingly sordid in the past sixty or so years.

"Well," she managed to say, "since we're not familiar with this particular soap then we don't have any emotional involvement with the characters, so what they're doing isn't particularly interesting."

"I wouldn't say that," Rafferty said critically, as the man began to move down the woman's body.

"Change the channel."

He gave her a charming, helpless smile. "I don't know how this thing works," he said, holding up the black keypad.

"Oh, for heaven's sake!" She jumped up and pushed a button on the oversize television, only to have the screen filled with still another couple, this pair fully dressed, sinking onto a sandy beach.

She pushed the button again, and a game show appeared, full of noise and flashing lights and cheering crowds. Rafferty glanced at her flushed face and considered seeing whether he could make the little black box work, then decided against it. She was still capable of kicking him out.

"You don't like love scenes?" he asked comfortably enough, setting the machine down on the cluttered coffee table.

"That's not it."

"You don't like sex, then?"

"That's not it, either."

"You do like sex?" He couldn't resist teasing her, even knowing it was dangerous.

"Rafferty..." Her voice carried just enough warning. "I'm going to work in my room. You can watch anything you please. We'll have to figure out how much time to allow to get to the Morettis . . .''

"Fifteen minutes. I know a shortcut."

She stared at him for a moment. "For someone who doesn't spend much time in Chicago you certainly seem to know your way around the city."

"Not really. They keep changing the streets, making them one-way when it's not the way I want to go. But I get around okay. I'm a good driver."

"You're atrocious," she said flatly. "I'll be ready to go by five-thirty. I believe in being prompt."

"Yes, ma'am."

"In the meantime, I have the yellow pages by the phone. You might make a few calls and find yourself a place to stay."

"Yes, ma'am," he said again, mocking her.

She walked out of the room without a word. A moment later he heard the bedroom door shut over the noise of the game show. He lounged on the sofa, not moving, as he thought about her.

With any luck he'd have to go wake her up. With any luck neither of them would leave that bed. Billy would understand. He'd been shocked as hell to find Rafferty there with her, and he'd taken Rafferty's terse account of Drago's attempt with both fear and fury. "You can't leave her, Rafferty. Not until we do something about the situation."

"I'm not about to leave her, Billy. Not until I have to."

And both of them knew when that moment would come. By the dawn of February 15.

Chapter Five

Helen Emerson had made some stupid moves in her life, but getting back into a car with Rafferty had to be one of the most spectacular ones. There was only one more idiotic action on her part, and that was wearing her black dress.

She knew about that dress—she couldn't fool herself into thinking it was accidental, couldn't even pretend it was the only thing she had to wear. Her brother Harry had told her that dress ought to be declared illegal, and he wasn't far wrong. She hadn't even dared wear it in her father's presence.

For one thing, it was much too short. Two inches above the knee, and even wearing opaque black stockings didn't tone down the effect of her legs. She had good legs—she considered them her only claim to beauty, and she couldn't resist the temptation of letting Rafferty get a good look at them.

The dress was also snug across her narrow hips, and admittedly cut too low. She told herself she wasn't well endowed enough to make it indecent, ignoring the fact that the dress made her seem positively curvaceous. She put on the dress, defiantly, spruced up her makeup, sprayed herself with another spritz of perfume and walked out into the living room with the tallest pair of heels she owned.

Rafferty didn't move for a minute, turning his attention from a home shopping show to stare at her, and she remembered how unnerving she found his stillness. It was all she could do not to tug at her neckline, pull down her hem. "Is this too dressy?" she asked, trying to keep the nervousness out of her voice.

"No," he said, sitting up on the couch, his dark eyes watching her. "Mary'll like it." There was a deliberate pause. "I like it."

Belatedly she wished she'd put her hair up. At least she had her glasses on to offer some sort of protection, as he rose from the sofa, clicked off the television and started toward her.

She wasn't going to back up. He wasn't a threat, she reminded herself. She trusted him, even if he made her uneasy. "Are you sure this is a good idea?" she asked, the question surprising her.

His smile was wry. "I'd ask you what you meant," he said in that deep, still voice, "but I think just about everything involving you is a bad idea, for me at least, so I'll just give you an unqualified no. Nevertheless, Mary wants to thank you personally for dropping the charges, and a spaghetti dinner is the best way she knows how. She's even willing to put up with sitting across the table from me for a few hours to do it."

That was enough to distract her from his troubling statement. "Why wouldn't she want to sit across a table from you? Doesn't she like you?"

His voice was lightly mocking. "What's not to like? Mary's afraid of me."

"That's ridiculous," Helen said. "Why should she be afraid of you?"

Rafferty didn't say a word. He was doing it deliberately—she recognized that fact, even as she felt herself respond. He was trying to frighten her as well as Billy Moretti's pregnant wife, and it was a wonder he wasn't succeeding. Or maybe he was, unnerving her in ways he hadn't intended.

She pushed a hand through her thick mop of reddish-brown hair. "Give it up, Rafferty," she said with a commendable amount of asperity. "I've spent time with serial killers, rapists, sexual deviates, the absolute scum of the earth. I've seen killers who would make Hannibal Lecter seem slightly antisocial. You can't psych me out."

"Hannibal Lecter?"

"You didn't see *Silence of the Lambs?*"

"Never heard of it. Is it a movie?"

Helen shook her head, aware that the tension in the room had lessened slightly. "What planet did you just arrive from, Rafferty? Mars?"

He smiled then, and the tension sizzled right back through her nerve endings. A tension she recognized, even though she'd never felt it before, as being purely sexual. "Pluto," he said. "You gonna let me drive?"

"Not on your life."

He did it then, what she'd subconsciously been waiting for, knowing it was coming. He reached out and touched her, put his long fingers through her thick, reddish brown hair in a caress that was so subtle, so soft that she couldn't reprimand him. "Come on, counselor. I heard on television that you only go around once in this life, and you have to grab for all the gusto you can get. Now I haven't seen much gusto around, but I'd sure like to drive that ridiculous little car of yours."

She gave in, not quite knowing why. Afraid it was just too easy to give in to this man. "You've got to promise you'll drive a little more carefully," she acquiesced. "I'm too young to die."

"So am I, Helen," he said, his voice flat and emotionless. "So am I."

He did his best, she had to grant him that. Considering that his best was a speed better suited to the Indianapolis 500 than the city streets of Chicago, Helen simply clutched the door handle, closed her eyes and prayed. By the time the car jerked to an abrupt stop outside a neat-looking tenement building on the South Side, she realized she'd be unable to find her way back. She was doomed to one more ride with the madman behind the wheel.

"Wasn't that better?" he asked with innocent pride.

"Since we're still alive I guess it was all right," she said grumpily, unfastening her seat belt with shaking fingers and sliding out of the car. He hadn't bothered to fasten his in the first place, and she knew she ought to berate him. Considering her knees were still a little weak, she decided she needed to sit down on something that wasn't hurtling along the streets, and she needed a drink.

Billy met them at the door, a proud, anxious expression on his face. His hair was combed back carefully from his boyish face, his clothes were neat and worn and he had his arm around a very pregnant young woman. Helen took one look at Mary Moretti's round, calm face, and knew she'd made the right decision. Even when Mary's eyes slid past her, nervously, to glance off the tall man standing directly behind her.

The apartment was surprisingly large, with three rooms, including a spacious kitchen, absolutely spotless and sparsely furnished. Billy had her seated on a sagging old sofa that wasn't much worse than the antique in her own apartment, a glass of rough red wine in her hand, before she had time to think about it.

"Have you still got my suitcase, Billy?" Rafferty asked. "I'd give ten years off my life for a shower and a change of clothes."

To Helen's amazement Billy proceeded to choke on his wine. When he managed to catch his breath he glared at Rafferty. "It's in the bedroom. Help yourself."

"You left your suitcase here?" Helen asked. "How long has it been since you were in Chicago—a year?"

"Exactly," Rafferty said. "I travel light. Got any shaving soap?" He ran a hand over the faint stubble, and Helen realized with a trace of a shock that she rather liked it. She usually found the unshaven look pretentiously scruffy. With Rafferty it was definitely appealing. But then, despite her common sense, she was finding just about everything about Rafferty appealing.

"I'll find it for you," Billy said, following Rafferty into the bedroom with the air of a man about to give someone a piece of his mind.

"I'd better check on dinner," Mary said, turning toward the kitchen.

There was no way that Helen was going to sit alone in the shabby, immaculate living room and sip her wine. "I'll help," she said, heading after Mary with the not very noble intention of pumping the woman for information.

"But you're our guest," Mary protested.

"Nonsense," Helen said briskly. "Give me something to do and point me in the right direction."

"Well, maybe the salad..."

"I'm very good at salads," said Helen, who was a great believer in supermarket salad bars. "So how long have you and Billy been married?"

"Eight months," Mary said, suddenly looking pale. "The baby's due in late April."

"He'll be a big baby," Helen said offhandedly.

"Yes," Mary said with an effort. "Ms. Emerson, I wanted to thank you for dropping the charges against Billy. He's a good man, and there were circumstances, things he can't explain...."

"I understand," Helen said soothingly, though she wasn't sure she did. "I agree with you—he's a good man. I trusted my instincts. And Rafferty's."

Rafferty hadn't been exaggerating. The normally stalwart Mary Moretti looked definitely uneasy at the mere mention of Rafferty's name. "He's been a good friend to Billy."

"But you don't like him." Helen decided it was time for a little prodding.

"Oh, no!" Mary protested. "It's not that. He just makes me a little...uncomfortable. I guess it's those eyes of his. They look like they could see right through to a person's insides."

"You should ask him if you're going to have a boy or a girl."

Mary looked startled, then managed a weak smile at Helen's joke. "I'd rather be surprised. Besides, it won't be much longer."

"I hear the last month is the worst." Helen had seen enough pregnant women, including her sisters-in-law, to know that Mary was a lot farther along than seven months, unless she was preparing to give birth to triplets.

Mary's eyes met hers. "It is," she said.

"Are Rafferty and Billy good friends? They don't seem like they'd have much in common," Helen asked in her most offhanded voice as she began to shred the lettuce.

"They go back a long ways," Mary said nervously.

"It can't be that long. How old is Billy, twenty-three? Twenty-four?"

"Twenty-five."

"And Rafferty must be about ten years older. Did they work together?"

"I . . . I don't really know," Mary said, her voice sounding strained.

Momentary guilt swamped Helen. Mary Moretti had too big a load to carry, literally as well as figuratively, to be plagued by questions she either couldn't or didn't want to answer. But those questions were looming larger and larger in Helen's mind, and she knew she wasn't going to get a straight answer out of Jamey Rafferty.

"Tell me, how did Billy and Rafferty meet?" she asked in what she hoped was a nonthreatening voice as she reached for the bag of carrots.

There was no answer. She turned back, expecting Mary's nervousness about Rafferty to have silenced her, only to find her hostess leaning against the wall, her face dead white, her hands clutched to her swollen belly. "Oh dear," she said faintly.

"Oh, dear?" Helen echoed, not liking the sound of this.

"I guess they weren't false labor cramps after all. I think . . ." She took a shuddering, gasping breath. "I think my water's broken."

"Hell and damnation," Helen said, immediately putting her arms around Mary. "Let me get you to the sofa. Billy!" she called out, struggling under the pregnant woman's weight. "Rafferty, damn it, get out here!"

The door to the bedroom slammed open, and Billy came at a run, catching Mary as she sank onto the sofa. Rafferty was behind him, dressed in a pair of slacks, pulling a fresh white shirt around him. "She's in labor," Helen said. "We've got to get her to the hospital."

"It's too early!" Billy protested. "She's only seven months along."

"Seven months..." Helen started to protest, but Mary's hand reached up and caught hers, gripping it tightly. She looked down, into Mary's wide, beseeching eyes, and immediately swallowed her protest. "Seven months is just fine," she said instead. "Besides, it looks like it'll be a big baby."

"Call the hospital," Rafferty said. "I'll drive you in Helen's car."

"I'll drive," Helen shot back. "We want them to get there in one piece."

"If you drive, counselor," he said, pulling another dark jacket around his opened shirt, "we won't get there till Arbor Day. You want to be the one to deliver this baby?"

For a moment she was transfixed, distracted by the smooth, muscular column of his chest. She jerked her eyes upward to his face. "You drive," she said. "But be careful." She knelt down beside Mary, taking her cold hand. "You'll be all right," she murmured.

"It's Billy's baby, miss," Mary whispered, as Billy's nervous voice could be heard from the kitchen, talking into the telephone. "He's kind of old-fashioned, and we only... I mean, it was just once before we got married, and he'd hate to think his first baby was conceived out of wedlock. It was just a little lie...."

"Don't worry about it," Rafferty said evenly, his voice cool and matter-of-fact. "Billy probably doesn't know enough to realize the baby should be smaller. He comes from a place where men weren't that up on women's biological functions."

Helen glanced from Mary's blushing face to Rafferty's ironic one. "And just what sort of place is that?" she asked. "Is that where you came from?"

"I told you, Helen. Pluto."

Billy tripped on his way back into the living room. "They're waiting for us. They say we have to time the pains. I've got a watch somewhere..."

"Take mine." Rafferty stripped off his watch, but Billy just stared at it stupidly.

"Give it to me," Helen said, taking it away from him. "Let's get Mary out to the car. I don't think we have much time."

Billy was a slight young man, with skinny arms and chest, just about average height. When he tried to scoop his wife's heavy body into his arms he staggered backward.

With a sigh Rafferty stepped forward, taking Mary from him, and Helen listened to the woman's shriek of terror with abstracted curiosity. "He's not going to hurt you, Mary," she said. "He's just going to help get you to the hospital. Now calm down and tell me when the next pain starts so I can time it."

It started halfway down the wide front steps. Helen glanced at the watch, peering at the old-fashioned dial as the gold second hand began its sweep. A moment later she was in the cramped back seat of the car, with Mary's head in her lap.

It was just as well she was too busy timing Mary's contractions to notice the way Rafferty was driving. When she did glance up they were taking a corner on two wheels, as pedestrians scattered before them in terror. "Rafferty," she warned.

At one point she glanced out the back, into the dark city night. A light snow had begun to fall, and the wind was whipping through the streets. The traffic was heavy, with one dark sedan driving uncomfortably close to the back of Helen's car.

There was something oddly familiar about that car, and she wasn't sure why. She squinted into the darkness, trying to make out the shape of the driver, when Mary's moan pulled her attention back to matters at hand.

"Ms. Emerson," Mary moaned.

"For God's sake, call me Helen."

"Ask Rafferty to hurry."

He overheard her plaintive voice. "Like a bat out of hell, Mary," he called back over his shoulder.

"Shut up, Rafferty," Billy snapped. "I'm not in the mood for your sense of humor."

"Did I miss something?" Helen asked, failing to see the joke.

"I'll tell you when I know you better," Rafferty said, cutting the wheel sharply.

Helen opened her mouth to shriek a protest when she realized they'd stopped, just inside a hospital portico. "Thank God," she breathed, scrambling out of the car to make way for the emergency room staff as they bundled Mary out of the cramped back seat.

Rafferty caught her as she stumbled in her too-high heels. "Thank God because Mary got here in time?" he inquired. "Or thank God the drive is over?"

"A little of both," she said. His hand was resting lightly on her arm, and even through the heavy down of her coat she could feel the warmth of his skin. She should move away, she knew it. But she didn't.

At some point during their race from the apartment he'd managed to finish dressing. His shirt was buttoned, covering his chest, and he'd reknotted another dark tie around his neck. She stared at it for a moment. "Do you always wear a tie?" she asked, abstracted.

He smiled wryly. "Don't you like it?"

"It's pretty formal."

"Do you want me to take it off?"

She stared up at him. His hand was still on her arm, lightly, possessively. In the background Mary was being wheeled into the emergency room, and the orange and blue lights of an ambulance still flashed lazily over the waiting cars, but the two of them seemed locked in a cocoon of quiet, removed from the hubbub of the hospital. "You might be more comfortable," she suggested, half shocked at herself.

"Why don't you take it off me?"

She ran the tip of her tongue across her lips in an instinctive, nervous gesture. "I don't know how."

"You have brothers, don't you? You must have tied their ties for them. You just do the same thing. Only backward." His voice was low and seductive. "What's the matter, counselor? You chicken?"

She reached up and caught his tie. "You know, Rafferty," she said, yanking on it slightly, just enough for him to feel it, "You'd tempt a saint."

"I'm trying, Helen. I'm trying."

Her hands were clumsy with the perfect Windsor knot. He made no effort to help her, just stood there patiently, staring down at her, as she loosened his tie. "You might undo the top button as well," he suggested evenly.

His skin was warm beneath her hands. She could smell the tang of shaving soap and shampoo, and for a brief moment she wondered what his skin would taste like.

The notion shocked her enough to make her step backward, away from him. "There," she said briskly. "You look a lot more approachable."

"Do you want to approach me?"

"Give it a rest, Rafferty. I was thinking of Mary. I don't think she needs you frightening her any more than necessary, but Billy will need you around for moral support. You might at least try to look human for a change, instead of like some damned sphinx."

"Yes, ma'am," he said humbly. "Are you going to stay?"

The question startled her. "I wasn't planning on going anywhere. Unless I'm not wanted."

He looked down at her. "Oh, you're wanted, Helen. You're most definitely wanted."

She started to protest, then gave up as he took her arm and ushered her into the emergency room. Flirting seemed to be a second nature to him—he probably had no more romantic interest in her than he had in Mary Moretti. She glanced behind her, briefly, and for a moment she thought she saw the same dark sedan that had seemed to dog their path from the Moretti's apartment. But the car was parked, there was no driver in sight, and most dark American sedans looked the same to Helen.

Billy was holding Mary's hand as they wheeled her down the corridor. He cast a last, beseeching glance at Rafferty, who nodded mysteriously. "I'll take care of things," he called after Billy. "I'll take care of everything."

"Everything like what?" Helen demanded.

"Paperwork," Rafferty said. "Obligations. That sort of thing."

"What obligations do you have?"

"Any number of them. God, I'd kill for a cup of coffee. Even some as awful as the stuff you made me."

Helen managed a smile. "It was pretty awful, wasn't it? I bet whatever they have in the vending machines around here couldn't be any worse."

"They have coffee vending machines? What will they think of next?"

She stared up at him. There were times when she could almost believe he *did* come from another planet. "Trust me, Rafferty, coffee vending machines are no great boon to civilization. Wait till you try some."

She left him with the paperwork and went in search of a coffee machine. As she suspected, it actually managed to taste worse than the cup she'd nuked him at her apartment, but he drank it down almost absently, barely noticing, while he dealt with the officious admitting nurse.

"They don't have any insurance," Rafferty was saying patiently. "I thought I explained that."

"And I thought I explained that someone will need to guarantee payment," the junior-size Valkyrie replied. "Where's the father?"

"In the delivery room," Helen said, pushing forward. "I'm sure he'll come out and sign the necessary papers as soon as he can—"

"What do you need?" Rafferty interrupted her in midspate.

"A major credit card, at the very least," the woman sniffed.

"I don't carry credit cards."

Both Helen and the admitting nurse stared at him in shock. "Then a personal check," the woman said. "As a deposit against the bills."

"I don't have a checking account," Rafferty said calmly.

"Then just what do you have?" the woman demanded in a frosty tone of voice, obviously jumping to the conclusion that Rafferty was a deadbeat.

Helen decided to keep her mouth shut. Rafferty was more than capable of putting the woman in her place, and she found she was almost looking forward to it.

"Cash," he said.

"Cash?" the woman echoed, astonished.

"Folding money. Long green. You've heard of it, surely?" Rafferty said, pulling out his wallet. "How much do you want before you'll leave the Morettis alone?"

"We'll need a deposit of at least a thousand dollars. Even a normal delivery costs upwards of five thousand, and..." Her voice trailed off as Rafferty pulled out a neat stack of brand-new thousand-dollar bills. He dropped five of them on the counter in front of the nurse, then added an extra.

"That should take care of things."

"Is that real?" the woman asked in an awed voice.

"There isn't much future in counterfeit." He put his wallet away, turned to Helen and offered her his arm in that old-fashioned, mockingly polite way he had. "Let's see how Billy is doing."

Helen waited until they were out of earshot. "I've never seen a thousand-dollar bill before," she said, still bemused.

A sardonic smile curved Rafferty's mouth. "Haven't you? Then you've obviously been traveling in the wrong crowd."

"Where did you get it?"

He glanced down at her. "None of your business, counselor."

"Is it drugs? Are you a dealer?" She tried to pull away. There was only one reason for anyone to carry that much cash around, and her sense that Rafferty was a man living on the very edge only increased her fears. She'd been a fool to trust him, blinded by her insensible infatuation with the man.

He stopped in the middle of the busy corridor, and people had to thread their way around them. He looked angry, and Helen told herself she should be frightened. Instead all she felt was relief. "Let's get one thing straight, lady," he said in a tight, furious voice. "I may not have always followed the law exactly, and I may have done some things I shouldn't have. But I don't mess with the drug trade, I never have, and I never will. You got that straight?"

"Yes," she said in a quiet little voice.

"Do you believe me?"

"Yes," she said.

He continued to stare down at her for a long, measured moment. And then he nodded, satisfied. "Let's go find Billy and see if we can help him pace."

"I don't think he'll be pacing. He'll probably be coaching Mary."

"Coaching her? Coaching her to do what? She's having a baby, not playing football."

"Rafferty, what kind of vacuum have you been living in? Husbands assist their wives when they give birth, they hold their hands, they help them breathe, they don't pace the waiting room smoking cigarettes."

"He'll be in there? Watching?" Rafferty echoed, aghast.

"I expect so."

He shook his head in disbelief. "Let me tell you, Helen, Chicago is one weird place nowadays. I guess

I'll have to do the pacing for him. Unless we're supposed to go in, too?'' Clearly the idea appalled him.

''No, Rafferty. Only the father. Don't worry,'' she added mischievously. ''You can always hold my hand.''

It was the third mistake of the evening. He put his long fingers under her chin, tilting her head up. ''I'd rather work on helping you breathe,'' he said. ''Maybe a little faster. A little deeper. With a little catch in your voice, and...''

''Cut it out, Rafferty,'' she said, backing away nervously. The man's effect on her was astonishing. ''We have more important things to do.''

''Like what?''

''Like getting a baby born.''

He looked at her for a moment. ''That won't take too long. We'll talk about your heavy breathing later.''

Chapter Six

It was a long night. Rafferty did his best to uphold traditional family values, but the hospital refused to cooperate. Apparently no one, not even expectant fathers and expectant godfathers, were allowed to smoke on the hospital premises, and there wasn't even room to pace. He had to content himself sitting in a plastic chair, nursing cup after cup of horrible coffee, and looking at Helen Emerson. All in all, he'd spent far worse nights in his misbegotten life.

Damn, she was pretty. He didn't know why he hadn't realized it right away. She had the most beautiful eyes he'd ever seen, warm brown with just a trace of defiance. He kept thinking about her mouth, too. Whether she'd kiss him back when he finally kissed her. Whether she'd use her tongue.

He wanted to thread his fingers through her thick brown hair, tilt her face up to his and find out. He knew now that she had breasts, and legs, and hips— that luscious little dress had cleared up any of his previous misconceptions. He loved watching her in it. He was looking forward to watching her get out of it even more.

Billy staggered into the waiting room at half past eleven, pale, sweating and faintly green as he collapsed into a chair. "I don't know about this, Rafferty," he muttered. "I think I like it the old-fashioned way, where the women do all the work."

Helen's laugh was unsympathetic. "Sorry, mister. You were there in the beginning, you need to see it through. At least it doesn't hurt you."

"But it does," Billy said earnestly. "Every time one of those pains hit Mary I can feel it in my own gut."

"Trust me, it hurts her more than it hurts you," Helen said.

"How many babies have you had?" Rafferty asked her.

He even liked the faint color that mounted her cheeks. "Lots of nieces and nephews," she replied, meeting his gaze levelly.

"Got to get back there," Billy muttered, surging to his feet again and heading toward the swinging doors of the delivery ward. "Keep the coffee hot."

Rafferty watched him leave. "It might taste better cold," he murmured.

"It couldn't taste worse," she murmured, aiming for a casual tone. "How did you and Billy happen to meet?"

He stretched his legs out in front of him, surveying her coolly. "Ms. Emerson, I've been pumped for information by the best of them, and your technique doesn't cut it."

"I'm not pumping you," she said, affronted. "I was just making conversation."

"Then let's talk about you. About your family of cops, about why you're a state's attorney, about where you went to school, about why you're not married, or even involved with someone."

She flushed. "What makes you think I'm not involved with someone?"

He watched her. "If you were involved with someone he wouldn't be fool enough to leave you without a date on a Friday night. For that matter, he would have been at your apartment when I arrived at six o'clock this morning. Unless you're involved with a jerk, and you strike me as too smart a lady to be involved with an idiot."

"There's no accounting for tastes," she said gloomily.

He let his gaze slide over her, the long legs, the virginal mouth, so very different from Crystal Latour and any other woman he'd ever been with. "I agree," he said. He glanced behind him. He'd had the strangest feeling, ever since they'd arrived at the hospital, that someone was watching. He'd learned to trust that sixth sense over the decades that had constituted his stop and start life, but this time he couldn't find anything or anyone to account for it.

It could only be Drago, though how he followed them, and where he was at that moment, was anybody's guess. The one time Ms. Emerson wanted to go the ladies' room Rafferty had skulked outside the door, looking like a pervert, until she emerged. There were too damned many people scurrying around this hospital, and the sooner Mary had her damned baby and he got Ms. Emerson safely out of here, the better.

James Rafferty Moretti made his appearance at 12:53 a.m., Valentine's Day. Billy staggered out into the waiting room, a dazed expression on his face, and Rafferty caught him as he collapsed.

"It's good, Jamey," Billy muttered, momentarily oblivious to Helen's curious presence. "To be born on today of all days, it somehow makes it right, doesn't it?"

Rafferty was a cynical man, one who didn't believe in coincidences or redemption. He thumped Billy on the back. "It sure does, Billy."

"We're naming him after you," he said, wiping the dampness from his red-rimmed eyes.

"How much did you have to threaten Mary for that one?" Rafferty asked dryly.

"No, she agrees. You know Mary, she's just a little nervous around you. You can't blame her . . ."

"I don't blame anyone," he said.

"Do you mind? Us naming him after you?" Billy asked, suddenly anxious.

"No, Billy. This way, at least something of me gets to stick around after Valentine's Day."

"What do you mean by that?"

Damn, he'd forgotten about Helen and her inquisitive little mind. He turned to her. "Just that I've got to get back to where I came from on Sunday. I never get to stay too long."

"And that suits you?"

"Let's just say I'm used to it. Billy, we need to celebrate!"

Billy was weaving slightly. "I need to sleep. They're moving Mary and James to a private room. I don't know how we're going to afford it...."

"It's taken care of, Billy. Don't worry about it."

"Rafferty, are you sure?"

"I'm sure. I'm going to take Ms. Emerson home. She looks about as dead as you do. Give Mary my love, and tell her thanks."

"But I want to see the baby," Helen protested, as Rafferty caught her arm.

"You can see him tomorrow...."

"After waiting this long, I'm not leaving until I see him," Helen said stubbornly.

He knew she'd be stubborn, known it from the moment he met her. He turned back to Billy with a weary sigh. "Does this crazy hospital allow it?"

"I don't know," Billy said. "But I'll sneak you in."

He had to grant it to Mary Moretti—she was a fighter. She lay in the pristine white hospital bed, circles under her eyes that made her look like a raccoon, pale and exhausted and utterly radiant. She was even able to look at him without flinching, and he knew from experience just how hard she found that.

Helen was cooing and fussing over the wrinkly red scrap of humanity that the Morettis had just brought forth. Rafferty glanced toward his namesake, and the little creature let out an astonishing howl. "He's got your lungs, Billy," he said wryly. "And Mary's reactions."

"No," Mary said, obviously steeling herself. "We want to thank you, Rafferty. For everything you've done for Billy, but especially for right now. We want you to be little James's godfather."

"I always fancied myself a godfather," he murmured with a wry smile.

"Rafferty." Billy's voice carried its own warning, and Rafferty controlled his irreverence.

"I'd be honored, Mary. But you know I won't be here for his christening."

Mary, who knew exactly where and what he would be, nodded. "You'll be back next year. We'll do it then."

He smiled down at her, keeping his expression entirely devoid of mockery, and for the first time Mary didn't flinch. She smiled back, tentatively, and he nodded.

"I'm going out in the corridor," he said. "I don't think all this company's good for my little namesake. Say your goodbyes and leave the new family in peace, counselor."

"I'll be there in a minute," Helen said, still staring at the fussy little newborn with rapt adoration.

The corridor was deserted when he stepped out, closing the door silently behind him, deserted except for the white-coated orderly sorting things on the meal tray. The lights were turned down low, and it took Rafferty a moment to wonder why people would be having a meal at a little after one in the morning.

"Hi, there, Jamey." Drago's dark crazed eyes met his from across the cart. "Long time no see."

Jamey didn't move. He was blocking the doorway, and if he knew Helen Emerson, and in less than twenty-four hours he'd begun to know her very well, she wouldn't be making any haste to follow him. Particularly since he told her to. There was no need for him to panic.

"Drago," he said, acknowledging him.

"Morris," Drago corrected him. "You forget, I've got my new life. My happy, productive new life."

"I'm sorry about your wife."

Drago shoved the cart against the wall, the sound sharp and violent in the hushed hallway. "Why don't you just take a little walk, Jamey? I never liked you, but I'm willing to overlook that fact if you make yourself scarce. After all, we went through a lot together." Drago giggled, the sound boyish and eerie. "There's nothing like sharing a violent death to create a little male bonding. You heard about male bonding, Rafferty? Like in the beer commercials."

"Leave the Morettis alone, Drago."

"Oh, I will." He stepped away from the cart and advanced on Rafferty. He was a slight man, wiry, with a nervous, edgy way about him, always fidgeting, always moving. He looked no different than he had the morning of February 14, 1929. Except his eyes were a little madder. "It's your girlfriend I'm after. Don't go thinking she's finally going to be your salvation. I'd think after sixty-four years you would have given up on the notion of finding true love. Let's face it, Rafferty, you just aren't lovable.'' Drago giggled again.

Rafferty shrugged. ''Apparently not. I'm not expecting redemption from Helen Emerson. I'm just trying to keep her safe.''

''Forget it, pal.'' Drago rocked back and forth on the balls of his feet. ''There's nothing you can do to stop me. I'm going to finish her off. I have to. And as long as you're a modern-day zombie you can't do a thing. Here.'' He reached out his hand. He held a gun there, a snub-nosed, very lethal gun modern enough for Rafferty not to recognize the caliber. ''Why don't you try it?''

''I'm not interested in games, Drago. Leave Ms. Emerson alone. Find some other game to play.''

Drago shook his head slowly, his eyes darting over Rafferty's shoulder as the door behind him began to open. ''Sorry, pal. I've got to finish the story. She's got to pay for what she did. I'm a man who never forgets what's owed him. You remember that.''

Rafferty reached behind him, catching the door latch in his hand, pulling it tight. He remembered, all right. Drago had a capacity for violence and revenge that had made him a legend in a time when such stuff was ordinary. ''Leave her alone, Drago. Or I'll...''

''You'll what, Rafferty?'' Drago taunted. ''There's nothing you can do to stop me, and you know it. As long as I'm alive and you're still in your own personal limbo you can't do a thing to me. You can't shoot me, stab me, I bet you can't even call the cops on me. I'll be there when you least expect it. You got in the way yesterday, but you won't always be around. Maybe I'll just wait till the fifteenth. She'll be all mournful, wondering why you just up and left her without a word, and she won't even know what hit her."

She was pulling at the door with all her strength, yanking at it, while he held on just as tightly. "Get the hell out of here, Drago."

"Why don't you let the little lady out, Jamey? Let her face her nemesis?"

"You're crazy..."

"That's nothing new, Jamey." Drago laughed softly. "I always was."

With a final jerk Helen hauled the door open, stumbling into the hallway and falling against Jamey. He caught her arms, shielding her with his body, shielding her from seeing and recognizing Drago, shielding her in case Drago decided to shoot after all.

"What's wrong with you, Rafferty?" she demanded, pulling away from him and tugging her hemline down. She glanced down the corridor, at the white-coated figure disappearing around a corner. "Was that the doctor? Is there something wrong with Mary or the baby?"

"That was just an orderly, trying to throw us out," he lied easily, casually. "It's starting to snow out there. Put your coat on, counselor, and I'll get you safely home." At least he hoped he could. A man determined to kill Helen Emerson would wait until her bodyguard made his forced exit on February 15. But Ricky Drago wasn't a sane man. And he didn't look like a man who was willing to wait much longer.

The car was where he'd left it, adorned with a parking ticket. Rafferty scooped it off the windshield and tore it in half before he opened the door for the uncharacteristically silent Ms. Emerson.

"I'm going to have to pay that ticket," she said with an attempt at severity that only sounded sad.

"Come on, counselor. A lady in your position should know how to fix a parking ticket," he said, coming around and sliding into the driver's seat before she had a chance to realize she'd been outmaneuvered. "You should have learned that your first day in law school."

"We don't 'fix' tickets in Chicago, Rafferty," she snapped.

"Then things have changed even more than they seemed to." There was no sign of Drago when he pulled out in front of an oncoming ambulance, veering out of the way just in time, but he couldn't be too careful. He stomped on the gas, and the puny little engine jumped forward, sending them surging across the wide street, directly in the path of an oncoming truck. Helen shrieked and covered her face with her hands, Rafferty deftly missed the huge vehicle, and started a mad race down the broad, almost empty boulevard.

While she continued cowering he turned on the car radio, breathing a sigh of pleasure as the unexpected sound of hot jazz came over the speaker. Reaching into his pocket for his cigarettes, he plugged in the lighter, hoping to get a reaction out of his passenger.

She emerged long enough to glare at him. "No one's in labor right now, Rafferty," she pointed out. "You don't have to break the speed limit."

"I wondered when you were going to come up for air. Mind if I smoke?"

"Yes."

He'd already lit the cigarette, so he contented himself with smiling at her. No one was following them—for now Drago seemed willing to wait. "Cute baby," he said in a conversational tone of voice.

"Don't give me that, Rafferty, you barely looked at him," she said shrewdly. "I want the answers to a few questions, and I want them now."

"Do you? Am I being charged with a crime, officer?"

"Don't give me that, Rafferty. I want to know what's going on. Why did you keep me from coming out into the corridor? That was no orderly—I couldn't place him, but I know I've seen that man before. And what were all those veiled references to you leaving and coming back? Why can't you stay for the baby's christening? Why won't you come back for another year? How come you have thousands of dollars in cash in your wallet and no credit cards, no checking account..." A sudden horrifying thought struck her. "You *do* have a driver's license, don't you?"

"Yeah, I have one." It expired in 1931, but he didn't think she needed to hear that. She was already asking far too many questions as it was. And he was too busy trying to figure out how to avoid answering them, and how to finagle his way into her apartment for the rest of the night.

"Well, Rafferty? Are you going to give me any answers?"

"Lady," he said wearily, "you wouldn't believe me if I told you."

"Why don't you try me?"

That was exactly what he was longing, dying to do. She didn't even realize the double entendre, she was so caught up in her questions and confusion. He pulled to an abrupt stop, turning off the car. He didn't know what to say to her. A thousand things crossed his mind, such as, "Look, lady, you're in danger," to telling her he was a man who'd been dead for sixty-four years. Neither of those stories would sit too well with the pragmatic Ms. Helen Emerson. He was better off with his usual lies.

"I've got a demanding job," he said. "I get to Chicago once a year, for no more than forty-eight hours, and then I'm gone. I didn't keep you from coming out into the corridor—the door must have been stuck. I don't know the orderly—he was just some guy. And the money in my wallet's relatively clean, if any money can be called clean. Look at it this way, Helen, you make your living off drugs and prostitution, the same as Al Capone does."

"Did," she corrected sharply. "And he made his money trafficking in those crimes, in human misery."

"And you make your money trying to stop them. Let's face it, without organized crime you'd be out of a job and on the streets. And what do you think paid for that building you're living in? You think Crystal Latour inherited it from her rich uncle? Sugar Daddy is more like it. It's a dirty world, princess, and a dirty city, and you should know that as well as anybody. So don't start giving me the third degree like you've got some sort of right, because you don't have any. I'm not under your jurisdiction, I don't have to answer to you. I'm just trying to do the best I can in the short time I'm here.''

He stopped, abruptly, and silence filled the car. The streetlight outside didn't penetrate the interior of the little sedan, and he couldn't see her expression, couldn't even guess her reaction. He'd blown it. She wouldn't let him anywhere near the door to her apartment now, and he'd be forced to spend the night in the cold, watching from a distance to make sure Drago didn't decide to pay a little call.

"Are you going to take me home?" she asked finally in a subdued little voice.

"We're already here."

She craned her head forward to peer outside the window, and he could see her face. See the faint, shocking sheen of tears behind the thin, wire-rimmed glasses. "So we are," she said, reaching for the door handle.

He put out a hand to stop her. "Aren't you going to ask me in for coffee?" he said, admiring his own gall.

She laughed then, a rusty little sound. "You must have a death wish."

"What do you mean?"

"Anyone who'd willingly drink my coffee must be suicidal."

"Trust me, Helen, if there's one thing I'm not worried about, it's death." He hesitated, she hesitated. "Are you going to ask me in?"

"It's not a good idea."

"Probably not. I haven't got a hotel room. I suppose I could go back and spend the night at the Morettis."

"That would be the smartest thing," she said, not making any effort to leave.

"I don't want to."

She took a deep, shuddering breath. "I don't know what you're used to, Rafferty, but I'm not it. I'm not someone you can sleep with, then disappear two days later. I'm not made for casual sex."

"I know that."

"Then I don't think..."

"I'm not asking for sex, Helen. I'm asking for a place to spend the night."

Silence again. "You don't want me?" she asked in a quiet little voice.

"Counselor, I would give twenty years off my life, if I had them, to take you to bed tonight. But frankly, I've had a lot of women in my time, and I know when a woman's ready for a tumble, and when she's not. You're not. I'd like to spend the night on your sofa, drink your god-awful coffee in the morning and take you to see the baby again when visiting hours start. I don't want to spend the night in some anonymous hotel room, watching home shopping on the TV."

"I thought you liked home shopping."

"A little goes on a long way. What do you say, counselor? If I promise to keep my wild desires to myself, will you let me stay?" He practically held his breath, waiting. He didn't want to spend the night on the streets, watching her windows. He didn't want to spend the night on her sofa, either, but at least it would be comparatively warmer. Though not as warm as it would be in her bed.

"All right," she said finally. "But if my brothers ever hear about this they'll skin you alive."

"Trust me, Helen. I don't spend much time gossiping with cops."

There was no sign of Drago as he followed her up the front steps of Crystal's old building. No sign of anyone, and yet he could still feel that odd, prickling feeling on the back his neck. Drago was nearby.

Damn it, it wasn't fair. Drago was right—there was no way Rafferty could stop him if push came to shove. All he could do was keep Helen Emerson out of his range, and he could only do that for his short, allotted time span. Billy could do something. But if Billy managed to take Drago out before Drago got to him, he'd face charges of murder.

Hell and damnation. Why couldn't he be like other people, simply stay dead once he was killed? Why did he have to come back to troubles like these, impossible troubles? Why did he have to come back to a woman who disturbed his equilibrium, scraped his nerves, fired his libido and generally drove him crazy?

He did a subtle reconnoiter of the apartment, making sure every entranceway was locked and barred. If Helen noticed his edginess she was too nervous herself to comment on it. His next step was to turn on the television. Home shopping was finished for the night, and an old Humphrey Bogart movie was playing. One that still looked strangely modern to Rafferty's eyes.

"I love that movie," Helen said wistfully.

"Stay up and watch it with me," Rafferty suggested. "I'm not tired."

"I am."

"Just tell me what's happened so far."

He was doing it on purpose, but thank heaven she was too tired to realize it. She sank onto the sofa, curling her long legs underneath her, and took off her glasses, rubbing her eyes. "He's an ex-sailor, Lauren Bacall's the widow of a friend. Edward G. Robinson is a gangster, sort of like Al Capone."

"He doesn't look like Capone."

"Oh, I don't know. I've seen some pictures..." Helen said, yawning, her defenses beginning to slide.

Rafferty sat on the opposite end of the sofa, not close enough to scare her away. She glanced up at him, a skittish expression in her eyes for a moment, and then she leaned back. "He doesn't," Rafferty said.

"Anyway," Helen said sleepily, "they're on one of the Florida Keys. *Key Largo*—that's the name of the movie. And a hurricane is coming." She yawned, and her eyes fluttered closed for a moment, then opened again. "And the gangster is trying to get back into the country after he was deported..." She snuggled down lower in the sofa. "Just watch for a bit, and then you can ask me questions."

He watched, all right. He watched her. She was already asleep, her long eyelashes fanned out against her pale cheeks, and her long thick hair was tangled around her face. He reached out and took the glasses from her limp hand, then held them up to his own face. They were practically clear glass. Typical Ms. Emerson, looking for all the defenses she could find.

It would take more than clear glasses to protect her from the likes of Ricky Drago. It would take more than a family of cops.

Somehow or other Rafferty had to find a way to stop him, before it was too late. Or next year, when he returned, Helen Emerson would be gone.

Chapter Seven

Rafferty didn't want to sleep. When you only had forty-eight hours a year to live, you didn't want to waste it in bed. Alone, that is.

He rose from the sofa, kicked off his leather wing-tips and headed into the kitchen. He found the almost empty coffee jar but nothing as useful as a kettle. He wasn't going to risk the microwave—it still looked like something out of Buck Rogers to him, and he didn't want to risk waking Helen up by exploding the kitchen. He boiled some water in a saucepan, scraped the hardened crystals into a mug and drank the brew down without shuddering. He'd done tougher things in his life. But not many.

Ms. Emerson wasn't a great believer in food. He found cans of soup and a half-empty box of crackers, two things that hadn't changed much in the past sixty-some years. He stood in the kitchen while the soup heated, staring out the window into the darkness. Somewhere out there Drago waited. Somewhere nearby. And it was a cruel twist of fate that a maniac like Drago had the ability to maim and kill, and Rafferty was helpless to stop him.

It made a kind of cosmic logic, one of the Scazzetti brothers had pointed out the second year they'd come back. If whoever was in charge of sending them back had any sense, he wouldn't allow felons back into society with the ability to continue committing crimes. They were getting a second chance all right, but the deck was stacked.

Which had been fine as far as Rafferty was concerned. Working for Moran had been a job, no more, no less. An exciting job, a dangerous job, a well-paid one. But not on the order of a religious calling.

Besides, with only forty-eight hours, he didn't have to worry about earning a living. Particularly when he returned each year with exactly what he left with. A package of Black Clove gum, a crumpled pack of cigarettes and a wallet crammed full of very crisp thousand-dollar bills that was supposed to pay for a shipment of Canadian bootleg liquor.

He leaned against the sink and closed his eyes, remembering Drago's malicious words. Maybe he just wasn't very lovable. During the intervening decades all of the others had found someone to love them, found a new life with all the trials and joys inherent. Even Drago seemed on his way to a decent life until fate once more stepped in.

But it hadn't happened to Rafferty. Of the seven men killed in that garage on that wintry February day, he was the one with the least on his conscience. The others, even Billy, had been involved in enforcing

Moran's rule, in resisting Capone's efforts to take complete control. Rafferty had stayed out of that side of things.

But in the long run he was the one who was still paying. The others had made peace with their past and found new lives. Not Rafferty.

He'd come close a few times. Most particularly in 1946, when he met a smart, sweet woman named Carrie who fell in love with him. He believed her when she said she did. He believed her enough to ask her to marry him, and they set the date for February 16. But he wasn't around then.

He could have been happy with her, he knew it. But he hadn't had that chance. By the following year she was gone, moved back to her hometown in Indiana and Rafferty had realized that the rules didn't hold for him. He wasn't going to get out of this endless cycle, and the sooner he accepted that fact, the sooner he began to enjoy what he had, the better.

But Ms. Helen Emerson was stirring old feelings inside him, old and new. He was drawn to her, in ways he couldn't remember being drawn. And while he wanted nothing more than to strip off that clinging little dress and teach her about her body and his, something stopped him. The knowledge that he wouldn't be there in the morning. Sure, this morning he'd be there. But not the next. And for all the toughness she tried to project to the outside world, inside she was nothing more than a soft, vulnerable kitten. And he never hurt helpless creatures.

He didn't even taste the soup and crackers. When he walked back out into the living room the television was flickering, the movie long gone. Helen had shifted in her sleep, stretching her long, silk-clad legs out in front of her, and the short black dress rode higher, halfway up her shapely thighs. Rafferty looked at her and stifled a groan.

He could move silently, and he did so, rummaging through her bedroom, not quite certain what he was looking for. He tried to keep his eyes from the bed. Thank God it wasn't the same one he'd once shared with Crystal Latour, but it was almost as bad. The brass-and-iron headboard was adorned with fat cupids, and the pile of fluffy white covers looked both virginal and enticing. Why the hell did he have to get mixed up with someone like Helen Emerson?

He found an ivory afghan in a closet that was filled with the same, shapeless men's clothes she'd been wearing when he first met her. He found the loaded gun in her desk drawer.

He wondered if she knew how to use it. Probably. With a protective family of cops behind her, she would have been given more instruction than the average rookie. She'd probably be a better shot than he was. He'd never been crazy about guns, even though he'd carried one, and used one, out of necessity.

Hell, who was he kidding? Of course she'd be a better shot, considering the fact that if he tried to cock it and pull the trigger the damned thing would simply refuse to fire.

He used to wonder if the same thing would happen if he pointed it at his own head. If there was a way out of this endless cycle.

But that wasn't his style. He didn't believe in weakness, or self-pity. If he was doomed to come back year after year then he could just make the best of it. Enjoy what pleasures were offered him.

The only problem was, Helen Emerson wasn't offering him any pleasures. And he wasn't about to take them.

He tucked the compact little gun in his jacket. He wasn't quite certain why—Helen stood a greater chance of using it to keep Drago at bay, if things got that bad. But he couldn't bring himself to let go of the small sense of power it gave him.

She didn't move when he draped the white coverlet over her body, covering her long, luscious legs, her surprisingly curvaceous body. She sighed, snuggling deeper into the soft old sofa, and he stood there, staring down at her.

A strand of hair had fallen over her face, caught against her lower lip. He wanted to see her face. He reached out a gentle hand and took the thick lock of hair, moving it away from her mouth. And then he let his fingers trail, feather light, against her lips.

They moved against his skin. He didn't know whether she was saying something in her sleep. Or kissing him. He didn't want to know.

He didn't trust himself on the sofa with her, big as it was. He moved back across the room, sinking into the old chair, stretching his legs out in front of him and watching her. He wanted a cigarette, but he was afraid it might wake her. He wanted a drink, but he'd already ascertained that Ms. Emerson didn't carry anything more than a vinegary-smelling bottle of white wine, and after all these years he still had *some* standards.

He didn't want to sleep. But somehow, sitting in the darkened room, with only the glow of the flickering television set and the faint scent of Helen Emerson's perfume surrounding him, he began to feel at peace. It didn't matter that a crazy man was lurking outside, ready to kill the woman he'd decided to protect. It didn't matter that impossible desire was eating a hole in his gut. It didn't even matter that he'd gone more than an hour without a cigarette. Alone with Helen Emerson, he felt oddly serene. And within moments, he followed her into sleep.

He dreamed of Elena. He hadn't thought of her in years, had done his very best not to think of her. Even fifty-some years after her death, sixty-some years since he'd seen her face, her memory still had the power to bring forth emotions he wanted to stifle.

He remembered the first time he saw her. He'd been with Moran himself, an unwilling part of his entourage as he made a social call on a store owner on the South Side. The store owner hadn't been interested in buying Moran's watered-down liquor to sell under the counter, hadn't been interested in paying the alternative, a large sum for protection from Capone's rival organization. Rafferty had stood to one side, his face blank of all emotion, as Ricky Drago had systematically broken Giuseppe Petri's hands. Only making a move when his daughter had burst on the scene, screaming with rage.

Ricky would have killed Elena, given half the chance. He hadn't liked the fact that Rafferty had stepped between them, pushing Elena behind him. Most people were terrified of Drago's lightning temper and violence. But they were equally in awe of Rafferty's legendary control.

Moran had watched the stand-off with interest and amusement, finally calling Ricky off when it looked as if one of them would wind up dead. "Cut it out, you two," he'd said. "I need both of you too much to let you get into fights. If Jamey wants the girl, let him have her. God knows, he could probably use a little action on the side."

Drago had backed off, staring at Rafferty out of hate-filled, crazy eyes. And if Capone's men hadn't intervened on a cold Valentine's Day less than a year later, Ricky would have put a bullet in his head when he least expected it.

He'd watched as Moran and the others drove away. He'd been left with one of the Packards—Moran was a gentleman in such matters, and Rafferty drove Petri to the hospital himself, with Elena crooning comforting words to her father as she rode along.

He waited until Petri's hands were splinted and bandaged, waited until he'd paid the bill in full from the thick wallet of Moran's money he always carried, waited until he drove the two Petris back home and Elena got her father settled in bed.

And then he'd tried to kiss her.

Of course she'd slapped him. When he kissed her the second time she slapped him harder. When he kissed her the third time she kissed him back.

But it hadn't worked. Not with her hot-tempered father screaming imprecations at Moran's head and at anyone connected with him. Not with Elena's old-fashioned values warring with her undeniable passion for him. Not with the escalating gang war that had taken the Petris' store, their house and the life of Elena's younger brother.

He'd even offered to quit. To go away with her, from the city, from the gangs, from the memory of grief and blood.

And she'd told him no. Even as she told him she loved him, she kissed him goodbye on a cold February morning. "Not in this lifetime," she'd said, her husky voice filled with implacable sorrow. And he'd never seen her again.

She'd never married, he knew that. She'd died of meningitis a few years after the massacre, and he used to wonder if she ever regretted her choice, the values that he couldn't live up to.

Because he sure as hell regretted them. He'd loved that woman, with a mindless, blind passion, and he'd had it thrown back at him for failing to measure up. He'd vowed then never to make that mistake again. And he never had.

But still, every now and then he thought about Elena. She was very, very different from the uptight Ms. Emerson. Full of old-world values, Elena had been dependent on the men in her life, a dutiful daughter, a passionate lover, a grieving sister. She'd been short, and plump, and luscious, and she'd made no demands on him. Except that he be someone he wasn't.

He'd tried to keep away from good women ever since. It was a waste of his time, and time was one thing in short supply. He was stuck here with Helen Emerson, a far cry from either Elena or Carrie, but a good woman just like those two. And he wished to hell it was February 15, and he no longer had to think about it.

HELEN AWOKE WITH A START. It was pitch black, her back hurt, her bra was digging into her rib cage and she had to go to the bathroom. On top of that, she wasn't alone.

She didn't move, lying there trying to orient herself. It came back to her in stages. She was lying on her sofa, her skirt indecently high. Someone had covered her with her grandmother's afghan, and that someone was the other person in the darkened room: Rafferty.

She could see his shadow in the oversize chair by the window. He was asleep, soundly, she hoped as she carefully edged from underneath the cover. She tiptoed into the bathroom, closing the door silently behind her before turning on the light, and then stared at her reflection in shock.

She looked like a wanton, there was no other word for it. The knowledge should have distressed her, except for the fact that she looked like a very pretty wanton. She'd lost her glasses somewhere, but she didn't really need them, and her tangled hair, smudged makeup and clinging dress made her look sleepy and sexy.

Dear heavens, the man hadn't even kissed her, and yet all she had to do was be in the same room with him and she started thinking about things she'd never thought before. It was a good thing he was leaving in another day. If things went on this way she'd end up seduced and abandoned. And while the first part sounded delightful, the second wasn't nearly as appealing.

It was a fluke that she'd reached the advanced age of twenty-nine in a relatively pristine state, a fluke and the presence of her overprotective family. While she'd been brought up in the strict Catholic church of her ancestors, she'd always kept an open mind, and if she'd ever fallen in love with someone she would have made the next logical, physical step.

But she hadn't. There had been no one to set her heart to racing, her pulses to quivering, no one to cause that dull ache of longing in the pit of her stomach that had begun to plague her in the last twenty-four hours. No one but Rafferty.

Maybe it wasn't lust, maybe it was an ulcer, she told herself wryly as she washed the makeup off her face. Maybe it was the fact that for once her family wasn't there to scare the man away. Not that Rafferty struck her as the type who'd scare easily. If he wanted her, really wanted her, then the entire Chicago police force couldn't stop him. Only she could.

And she wouldn't. She knew that full well. The brief touches, on her back, when he'd taken her elbow, when he'd plowed into her on the sidewalk outside her office, still made her skin tingle. She wanted him to touch her again. Softer this time. And harder.

She shook her head at her reflection. She was crazy, there was no doubt about that whatsoever, and she could thank her lucky stars that Rafferty was both a gentleman and apparently uninterested in her, despite his protests to the contrary. She was perfectly safe with him. Damn it.

She turned off the light before creeping back out into the living room. Rafferty hadn't moved from his spot in the chair. His eyes were closed, his breathing deep and steady, and even if it was dangerous, she couldn't resist moving closer.

He wasn't the most handsome man she'd ever seen. His face was narrow, his mouth thin, his eyes, when they were open, were too mocking. But there was something about him that drew her, more intensely than if she'd been confronted with a combination of Kevin Costner and Richard Gere. Except that he reminded her more of Humphrey Bogart crossed with Cary Grant. With a touch of John Garfield on the side.

She reached out a tentative hand. A lock of dark hair had fallen on his forehead, and she pushed it back, lightly, carefully, letting her fingers skim his heated flesh for a brief moment. And then she moved away, out of harm's reach, out of temptation's way, stumbling over a pile of old newspapers as she went, banging into the wall, before she turned and ran, lightly, silently, into her room, closing the door behind her.

RAFFERTY WAITED until he heard the door close. He sat up in the chair, and cursed, silently, fluently, in words that hadn't changed in more than sixty-five years. Good Anglo-Saxon words that were probably around six hundred and fifty years ago as well.

It had been a close call. He'd woken the instant she had, keeping himself very still as she tiptoed into the bathroom. He'd never had a problem before, but when she'd approached him, when he felt the soft, minty sweetness of her breath, the feathery brush of her fingers on his face, he almost caught her wrist and yanked her down into his lap.

He wasn't a man of violent urges. But she brought violence out in him. He wanted to smother her, cover her with his body and push between her legs. He wanted to take her, in heat and passion and furious desire.

And he wanted to make love to her. Slowly, gently, seducing her away from her virginal fears, he wanted to bring her the kind of physical pleasure that would wipe everything else from her mind. So that when he left, she'd remember. Always.

But he'd controlled himself. And she'd backed away in time. Helen Emerson wasn't the woman for him. If he took her, he might as well let Drago finish her. She knew her needs very well—she wasn't the kind of woman for casual sex and brief affairs. She was a forever after kind of woman. And if he made love to her and then disappeared, a part of her would die. And he was man enough to control himself and keep that from happening. Wasn't he?

The problem was, he wanted her more than he'd ever wanted anyone in his entire life, up to and including Elena Petri. And the more he fought it, the more he needed her.

He rose, far more quietly than she had, and stretched out on the sofa. The cushions still held the imprint of her body. The afghan still held the trace of her scent. White roses. He'd never see a rose again without thinking of her.

He stared out into the darkened room, knowing that this time he wasn't going to sleep. This time he was going to lie awake and try to control his unruly body, try to control his unruly mind. He only had another twenty-four hours or less to get through. He could do it.

He stared at the blank television screen, wondering if he could find some more home shopping, maybe even one of those hour-long shows selling car wax. Anything to keep his mind off the woman in the next room.

But even the wonders of modern television couldn't distract him in his current state. All he could do was lie there on the sofa, imaging Helen beside him. And in the distance he could hear Ricky Drago's high-pitched giggle.

SATURDAY, FEBRUARY 14 dawned cold and blustery, not unlike another February 14 long ago. Rafferty watched the flakes of snow swirl down outside the window, and he thought about the woman in the other room. He hadn't been able to think of anything else for the past few hours of wakefulness, and the slow lightening of the city couldn't distract him.

Her scream echoed through the apartment, sharp, shrill, panicked. He surged off the sofa, kicking over the coffee table, yanking the gun from his waistband as he raced into her bedroom. If he couldn't stop Drago, maybe he could force her to pull the trigger.

She was alone, sitting up in the middle of that fluffy white bed. The curtains were drawn, there was no sign of any intruder. She simply sat there, her eyes wide with fear, her hands covering her mouth as if to stifle the screams. And then her eyes went to the gun he held in his hand, and the fear in her eyes turned to panic.

He put the gun down, carefully, on the dresser beside the door. "What happened?"

"A…a nightmare," she managed to choke out, still staring at him in shock. "I get them sometimes. They're…very real."

He stepped inside the room, knowing he shouldn't. "What did you dream this time?"

"It's always the same. I hear something that sounds like thunder. Or a thousand drumbeats. A roaring, terrifying kind of noise. And then nothing. Silence. And the howling of a dog."

Rafferty felt his skin crawl. He knew what she was talking about, even if she didn't. He'd been there.

He'd heard the thunder of the tommy guns as the bullets ripped into flesh. He'd lain there in a welter of blood, dying, and listened to the mournful howl of Scazzetti's old mutt, still chained to the wall, the only survivor of the St. Valentine's Day Massacre.

"It's just a bad dream," he said, hearing the harshness in his own voice. "Forget about it."

"But why does it keep coming back? Why can't I remember more of it? Why is it always the same? Why do I keep hearing that dog...?"

"Will you shut up about the damned dog?" Rafferty said savagely, crossing the room to the side of the bed. "It's just a dream. You must have read something about the massacre..."

"The massacre? You think I'm dreaming about the St. Valentine's Day Massacre?" she demanded, obviously astonished. "Why should I do that?"

He shook his head. He wanted to sit down on the bed beside her, he wanted to put his hands on her shoulders and draw her to him. She'd changed into some sort of oversize shirt; more men's clothes when he'd fantasized about white lace lingerie. He still found her irresistible. But he had to resist. He didn't move. "Beats me," he said, more calmly now. "But it sure sounds like your dream. The thousand machine gun bullets, and some old dog howling that finally brought help."

Her face paled. "You're kidding."

He shrugged. "You probably read about it and forgot. That's what the witnesses said about it. If it weren't for the dog howling no one might have checked for hours.''

He was unprepared for her reaction. He thought the simple truth would have reassured her. Instead she shuddered, making a small sound of infinite distress, and it was all the excuse he needed.

He climbed onto the high bed and reached for her, pulling her against him. She came readily enough, and he could feel the icy fear in her flesh, the terrified pounding of her heart beneath the thin cotton of her T-shirt. He'd just hold her for a moment, he told himself. He'd control himself, certainly he could do that. He'd just allow himself a minute of holding her, to calm her down.

And maybe one brief kiss wouldn't make things worse. He could brush his lips against her forehead, against the thick, sweet-smelling hair, and she might not even notice. It wouldn't do any harm. Even if he threaded a hand through the thick hair at the back of her neck, tilting her face up to his, it wouldn't cause irreparable damage. Even if she looked up at him, her eyes wide and solemn and waiting, her mouth pale and damp and slightly parted. He didn't have to kiss her, did he?

Yes, he did. He put his mouth over hers, and all his good intentions vanished. She had the sweetest mouth he'd ever tasted, shy, slightly uncertain, but more than eager. She slid her arms around his neck, kissing him back with enthusiasm that was astonishingly innocent, but then, he'd already figured she hadn't had that much experience. When he pushed his tongue between her lips she jumped, and he waited for her to pull away.

But she didn't. She simply clung more tightly, following his lead, her own tongue shyly touching his, until he thought he might explode with longing.

He pushed her down on the bed, covering her body with his, no longer caring about the consequences. Beneath the layers of fluffy white covers he could feel her body, slight and soft and trembling, and he wanted to push the covers away, strip their clothes away. He wanted to lose himself in her slender body and her wonderful mouth. He was tired of thinking about the consequences—he only had another twenty-four hours, damn it, and he wanted this woman, needed this woman, with a longing so fierce it made his bones shake. And she was shaking, too, with the same kind of need, and it made no sense whatsoever for him to reach his hands behind his neck and catch her arms, to pull them away, to break the kiss and move away from her, so that she looked up at him in wide-eyed shock and desire and frustration.

"You know as well as I do this is a bad idea," he said, surprised at the shaken sound of his own voice.

Neither of them moved. She still lay in the center of the bed, and he could see the rise and fall of her breasts beneath the soft cotton of her shirt. He didn't climb off the bed, as he knew he should. Some masochistic part of him made him stay right there, within reach, to prove he could do it.

"Why?" she asked finally, her voice small and brave.

"Because I'll be gone tomorrow morning. I don't want to be, but I don't have any say in the matter. And you'd be alone, figuring you'd been a fool, and you'd hate me, and even worse, you'd hate yourself."

"No, I wouldn't." She sat up, slowly, and she was too damned close to him. "Don't you know that people spend a lot more time regretting the things they don't do, and not the things they do?"

"Helen, you're not the type for a one-night stand. You're the kind of woman who needs commitment, who needs tenderness and a future. I can't give you any of that."

The small smile that curved her pale mouth was almost his undoing. "Why am I trying to talk you into this?" she asked. "Isn't it supposed to be the other way around?"

He made himself touch her, just to prove that he could, cupping her face with his hands and staring down at her. "Lady," he said, "I'll break your heart."

"My heart, Rafferty? Or is it your own you're worried about?" she said, humor warring with the faint trace of anxiety in her eyes.

It came to him then with the force of a blow. He could love this woman. This impossible, shy, fierce, brave woman, and the thought terrified him. Up until now he hadn't been that reluctant to leave when his time came, simply because he hadn't been leaving anyone behind. If he let himself care about her, love her, then leaving would destroy him. And he might see whether he could turn a gun on himself.

He smoothed the sides of her face with his thumbs. "I have no heart, Helen. No heart to break."

"Prove it," she said. And she kissed him, brushing her lips against his, lightly, lingering, and he knew he should pull away, but he couldn't. The sweetness of her mouth was more erotic than anything the professional Crystal Latour had ever come up with, and he slid his hands down her shoulders, down her arms, pulling her tight against him with a groan of despair.

She was unbuttoning his shirt, her hands clumsy and nervous and wonderful when they slid against his skin, touching him. She was pulling him down on the bed, and he told himself he'd been gentlemanly enough. Maybe she wasn't as inexperienced as he thought. There was one surefire way to find out.

He took the hand that had slid around his waist and pulled it down to the front of his trousers, to the row of tiny buttons that were straining over the effect she was having on him. He held her hand there, even as she tried to pull away, and he knew he hadn't been wrong.

He moved fast then, pulling away from her, climbing off the bed and standing at the far end of the room. His shirt was unbuttoned, he was having trouble catching his breath and his entire body throbbed. Damn her and her innocent eyes and her luscious mouth.

"Chicken," she said softly.

It was the final straw. If there was one thing James Sheridan Rafferty was not, it was a coward. He'd been about to button his shirt, but he left it hanging, reaching instead for the mashed pack of cigarettes that still survived. "No one calls me chicken."

"You must have seen *Back to the Future*," she said.

Her words gave him a start of surprise, before he realized she must be referring to a movie. "No," he said with a trace of wryness. "But I think I'd like it."

"Rafferty..."

"I'm not going to bed with you, Helen. Because I'm not going to be here tomorrow morning, and you deserve better than that." He tried to keep his voice flat and unemotional.

"Can't you call your boss and tell them you need a few extra days?"

He grimaced at the notion. "No."

"Can't you just miss your plane?"

"I didn't come here by plane."

"Well, how did you get here?" Helen demanded. "And for that matter, since we've already ascertained that you're not Billy's lawyer, what is it you do for a living?"

He looked at her. He'd never told a soul, never even been tempted. But he knew if he didn't come clean, didn't warn her exactly who and what he was, then he wasn't going to be able to resist.

He lit the cigarette, taking a deep, deliberate drag off it. "I don't do anything for a living, sweetheart," he said. "And I haven't for sixty-four years."

Chapter Eight

For a moment Helen didn't move. Her bedroom was shadowy, just the early-morning light filtering through her thin curtains providing some illumination, and she couldn't see his expression. Not that it would have done her any good. At his best, Rafferty was hardly the most communicative of men. Even in bright sunlight she probably couldn't guess what he was thinking.

"You want to run that by me again?" she said in an even voice. "That statement didn't make a whole lot of sense."

He was already regretting it, she could tell. She wondered what would happen if she pushed the covers aside. The T-shirt she was wearing only came to midthigh, and she already knew he was more than appreciative of her legs. She'd pushed it as far as she could go. For the first time in her life she wanted someone, she wanted Rafferty. She wanted him to show her what she'd been missing, to show her with love and gentleness.

But he frightened her. There might be love and gentleness, but there was also passion and a kind of darkness she didn't understand, and wasn't quite ready to face. So she kept the covers pulled over her, and waited.

"I'll make some coffee," he said. "If you want to hear about it, I'll tell you. But you won't believe me."

"Oh, I don't know," she said. "I've listened to a lot of unbelievable stories in my time. You could try me."

The suggestion hung in the air between the two of them, and there was no mocking smile on Rafferty's face. "I'll make the coffee," he said again.

"The coffee beans, if any, are in the freezer."

He stared at her blankly. "Why?"

"It keeps them fresher."

"Don't they grind coffee anymore?"

"It tastes better if you grind your own."

"I thought things were supposed to be getting easier," he muttered.

"What do you mean by that?"

"In the kitchen," he said. And he closed the door behind him when he left.

She dressed hurriedly, throwing on a faded pair of jeans and an old T-shirt before heading into the kitchen. Rafferty had found the coffee beans, but he was staring at them with dismay. "I don't see a coffee grinder."

She picked up her electric one, but he still didn't seem to recognize it. He hadn't rebuttoned his shirt, and it hung loose around his hard, muscled chest. He had a tan, and once again she wondered where he came from. Where he was going.

She took the beans from him without a word, making the coffee with brisk efficiency. She waited until it had begun to drip down into the pot, then she turned to face Rafferty, trying to find a place to focus her eyes. His chest was too distracting.

"Where'd you get your tan?" she asked, unable to keep from thinking about it. Wondering if the light sprinkling of hair would be rough or smooth against her hand.

"Florida. I was down there my last January."

"Is that where you're going when you leave here? Is that where you live?"

He shook his head. The kitchen was large for an apartment, but too small with Rafferty taking up space. The coffee dripped, slowly.

"Are we going to play twenty questions?" she asked sharply. "Or are you going to tell me?"

There was no warmth in his eyes, just a cold, bleak humor. "If you want to hear it. I don't know where I'll be. I don't know where I've come from. The tan on my body comes from my last visit to Florida, which happened to be in late January—1929."

She stared at him blankly. "So how old would that make you?" she asked, keeping her voice even.

"Depends on how you calculate it. I was born in 1895, in Columbus, Ohio."

"Which would make you ninety-eight years old. You're very well preserved," she said dryly. Drip, drip went the coffee.

"You could say so. I died when I was thirty-four years old. On Valentine's Day."

She didn't know if she could wait until the coffee finished. "Valentine's Day, 1929," she said. "Don't tell me. You were gunned down in a garage along with a bunch of other gangsters. And Al Capone was behind it."

"Yes."

She pulled out two mugs, her movements fast and jerky as she set them down on the counter. She pulled the pot out, listening to the hot coffee splash down on the burner, and filled both cups. She turned, holding her own mug in both hands, trying to hold on to something. "So what are you doing here?" she asked with what she considered to be admirable calm.

"Every year I return to Chicago for two days. February 13 and 14. And then I'm gone again. I don't know where I go in between, or what happens to me. Hell, I don't know if I really exist at all. Maybe I'm just a dream."

"A nightmare," Helen said, taking a sip of the too strong coffee to try to steady her nerves. "So what are you doing in my apartment?"

"That's a little hard to explain."

"Surely not. I mean, you haven't had any trouble giving me a pile of garbage about returning from the dead every year like something out of a bad movie. Why stop at this point?" Her voice was brittle, angry.

"You don't believe me?" He seemed more astonished than offended by the notion.

"Of course I don't believe you. I was never big on horror stories—*The Night of the Living Dead* isn't one of my favorite videos. Why are you really here, and what do you want from me? And what's Billy Moretti got to do with it?"

He hesitated, and she wondered if he was going to switch to the truth. Apparently not. "Billy was one of the men killed in the garage."

"Sure, Rafferty," she said in a brittle voice. "Then how come I've seen him any number of times and it wasn't anywhere near February?"

"He's come back for good. I haven't."

"Why not?"

"How the hell do I know? Maybe I'm worse than the others. Maybe I'm not deserving. Maybe..."

"Maybe you're full of crap."

Rafferty's eyes narrowed. He reached past her for his mug of coffee, and his long arm brushed hers. She could feel the tingle all the way to the pit of her stomach. Ulcer, she reminded herself. Not desire.

"You think I'm making this up?" he asked, taking a deep drink.

"I think you're probably a science fiction writer. That, or you work for 'Candid Camera.'"

"What's 'Candid Camera'?"

Something snapped inside her. "Don't give me that, Rafferty! You aren't some zombie gangster returned from the dead, and you aren't crazy enough to believe it. You're only crazy enough to think you ever had a chance of hell of convincing me."

Rafferty didn't move. That sense of stillness hovered around him, that unnerving quiet. And then he smiled, a wry, self-mocking smile. "You *did* strike me as extremely gullible," he said, taking another sip.

Perversely enough, now that he was admitting he lied she was starting to wonder whether there was any chance he was telling the truth. Then she gave herself a mental shake. "Why did you do it?"

"Do what?"

"Lie to me."

For a moment she hadn't been aware how close he was standing. He moved, leaning forward, and his body pressed against hers, pressed her back against the counter. She could feel the heat of his skin, the muscle and bone and sinew, she could feel how much he wanted her. He bent his head down and brushed his lips against hers, and he tasted of coffee, and cigarettes, and desire. "Because you're too tempting."

She let her lips cling to his for an instant, before drawing away. "And you're not a man who can resist temptation?" she whispered.

"I'm trying, counselor. I surely am trying." He pushed away from her then, and she suddenly felt cold. "What are we going to do today?"

"What's this we, white man?"

He stared at her in obvious surprise, but he made no comment, which was just as well. Everyone on this earth had heard the old Lone Ranger joke. Everyone, apparently, but Rafferty. "It's Valentine's Day, Helen. And as far as I can see, you don't have a line of eager young men ready to celebrate it. You'll have to make do with me."

"What are we going to do—visit the garage where you were gunned down?"

He shook his head. "It's long gone. There's a retirement home in its place, and I don't feel like visiting. Particularly since everyone in there would be younger than I am."

"Rafferty..." Her voice carried a very definite warning.

"I'll behave myself. Just pretend I never mentioned my scarlet past. I'm a dry goods drummer from Ohio, stopping over."

"Drummer?" she echoed, mystified. "Dry goods?"

"Salesman," he corrected. "In textiles and ready-to-wear clothing. I left my samples in the Packard..."

"Rafferty," she warned again.

"So how are we going to spend the day?"

She should order him out of the house. She should call the police, or the psychiatric ward, she should make some excuse and get the hell away from him. He'd done nothing but lie to her since she first met him, about Billy, about himself, about everything. And the odd thing was, the most outrageous lie of all was the most believable.

"I'm supposed to go to a party," she found herself saying.

He didn't look pleased at the notion. "Did you have a date?"

"It wasn't that kind of party. I have a bunch of friends who like to celebrate on an annual basis. They have an Oscar party every year, when we all wear evening gowns and eat popcorn and watch the Oscars. They have fireworks on the Fourth of July, they have Easter egg hunts where we all dress up in garden dresses."

"What do you do for St. Valentine's Day?"

She wished she hadn't opened her big fat mouth. It wasn't as if she believed him, even for one moment. But still, it felt tacky to explain. "We have a mock-gangster party in their garage," she said in a foolish little voice. "Everyone dresses up in 1920s' clothing and we drink rotgut liquor and listen to jazz and dance the Charleston."

"And then in the end everyone gets mowed down by tommy guns?" he suggested, his voice even, and there was no way she could read his reaction.

He had no right to a reaction, she reminded herself. He'd simply tried to fob a ridiculous story off on her. The annual day-long massacre party was a harmless spoof, and if Rafferty couldn't relate to that then he could take his tall, lean body and his sexy mouth and his deft, clever hands elsewhere.

"No," she said. "In the end everyone pairs up and goes out to dinner."

"And who were you planning to pair up with?" Lord, he sounded jealous. Another lie, of course.

She met his gaze calmly. "You," she said.

He closed his eyes for a moment, and she almost thought his expression was one of pain. And then he opened them again, and the mockery was back in full force. "Have you ever been warned about tweaking the tiger's tail, Helen? You may regret teasing me. I'm trying to be a gentleman, but I have very definite limits."

She wanted to push him past those limits. Or did she? She was no longer quite so certain. "Look at it this way, tiger," she said. "At least you won't have to come in costume. You already look the part."

She slid away from him, before he could say anything else. "I'm going to take a shower. Everybody has to be there by ten-thirty." She hesitated. "Aren't you going to ask me why?"

"I know why. That's when the massacre took place. You've got a tasteful bunch of friends, Helen."

"You don't have to come with me," she said, trying not to sound defensive.

"Yes, I do." He turned from her, staring out the window into the slowly lightening city sky. She watched him, the tall, straight back beneath the elegant white cotton shirt, the curl of dark hair at the back of his neck, and she wanted to go to him and thread her arms around his waist, to hold him tight against her. For whatever his reasons, he was going to leave, she had no doubt about that whatsoever. And she already knew she couldn't bear to let him go.

TELEVISION had lost the ability to charm Rafferty. While his tastes were catholic enough to include Saturday morning cartoons and ads for sugar cereal, he had too much on his mind to concentrate on the high-powered wonder of kids' TV.

He'd never made such a botch of something in his life. First, by kissing her. Second, by trying to tell her the truth. Of course she didn't believe him—who would? He hadn't even considered that possibility. He'd spent so many years not telling a living soul about who and what he was that he never thought they simply wouldn't believe the story.

He couldn't tell her about Ricky Drago. She'd already made it clear she didn't believe him—if he complicated matters by warning her about Drago she might kick him out for good. As long as he behaved himself she'd probably let him trail along after her.

He knew exactly how he needed to do it. He needed to flirt with her, just enough to keep her going, not enough to do anything about it. Flirting seemed to be a lost art nowadays, and he was out of practice, but a long time ago he'd been an expert. He'd become too cynical in the past few decades to be really good at it anymore, but when an attraction as strong as the one that blazed between him and Ms. Emerson existed it didn't take much to fan the flames.

His only mistake would be to give in to it. He'd come too damned close already, a fact that astonished him. He prided himself on being a man in control—of his emotions, which were nonexistent, his libido, which was too damned strong, and his temper. Since he had no control whatsoever on the rest of his life, he needed those small pieces of power.

But Helen Emerson stripped that power from him. She stirred emotions he didn't know still existed, she infuriated him and she made him feel as if he were a hormone-laden teenager, ready to jump on the first female that moved. Except that he didn't want to jump on any female but Helen.

Lord, this was getting worse and worse. It was bad enough that he was stuck spending his allotted two days on earth baby-sitting for an overage virgin. But then he had to go and fall in ...

He stopped that treacherous thought cold in its tracks. He didn't even believe in love. He believed in sex, and companionship, and even parenthood for those who were cut out for it. But true love went out with Romeo and Juliet. Look where it got people like Ricky Drago. Crazier than a bedbug, because he couldn't live without his dead wife.

That wasn't for the likes of Mrs. Rafferty's little boy Jamey. He'd made it this far without anyone. He could continue on that way, and be just dandy. As soon as he made sure Helen would be safe.

He was on his fourth cup of black coffee, his second episode of something bizarre called "Teenage Mutant Ninja Turtles" when Helen emerged from the bedroom. He looked at her, momentarily stunned.

She was wearing the kind of dress women wore when he was young. It was an off-white velvet chemise, studded with pearls, and her bare arms and neck were adorned with chains and beads. She was wearing white silk stockings, rolled to her knees with uncharacteristic daring, and her hair was pouffed and held back by a jeweled band around her forehead. Her eyes were lined with makeup, her lips and cheeks rouged and she looked like the woman of his dreams.

"It unnerves me when you do that," she said, tugging at her dress self-consciously.

Somewhere he found his voice. "Do what?" he asked.

"Stare at me like that." She did a nervous little pirouette, and he noticed she hadn't bound her breasts the way most women would have. The thought made him hard. "Don't I look like a gun moll?"

"No."

"No?" She tried for a pout, and almost succeeded.

"That's not a gun moll's dress. Where'd you get it?"

"From an antique shop. How do you know it isn't a gun moll's dress? I suppose you were intimately acquainted with them during your previous incarnation?" She was learning to be just as mocking as he was. If it wasn't so damned cute it would irritate the hell out of him.

"A few," he conceded, playing the game. "Including Crystal Latour."

That threw her for a moment. "You didn't!" she gasped, believing him.

"I did."

"That sweet old woman?"

"She was three years younger than me."

She stared at him in mute frustration, then shook her head. "You're good, Rafferty, I have to admit it.

You almost had me going there. So tell me, Mr. 1920s-gangster-expert, what kind of dress am I wearing?''

"A wedding dress."

She blushed. Damn, he loved it when she blushed. The color swept over her chest, up her face, even down her arms. "You're kidding!"

"All you need is a bouquet and a veil." He started across the room toward her, wondering if she was going to scurry away like a scared rabbit. She held her ground, but just barely, as he reached her, and she tilted her head back to look at him with just a trace of defiance. "You look perfect, counselor," he murmured, keeping his hands at his sides with the greatest of efforts.

"So do you," she replied, her voice husky. And she made the very great mistake of touching him, of putting her hands on the lapels of his suit, of moving close enough so that he could inhale the white roses in her perfume, so that he could feel the heat from her skin, and he couldn't help himself. He threaded his hands through her thick fall of hair and stared down at her with something close to desperation.

"I'm trying to do the decent thing, Helen," he muttered. "And you're making it impossible."

"What do tigers know about decency?" she whispered back. "Or dead gangsters, for that matter? If you really were who you said you were, you wouldn't think twice about seducing and abandoning me."

"Is that what you want?" Her mouth was too damned soft, too damned close to his.

"I don't want to be abandoned."

"Oh, damn," he groaned under his breath. And he couldn't do anything but kiss her.

She was already getting more adept at it. Her lips parted immediately beneath his, and she tasted of cherry-flavored lipstick and toothpaste, and she tasted of hope and innocence and love. And he wanted more and more and more.

She slid her arms under his jacket, around his waist, and then she grew very still, and cold, as her hands found the gun he'd tucked in his back.

She pulled out of his arms, and he let her go. "Why do you carry a gun?"

"It's yours."

"Why do you have it?"

He considered his possible responses, and took the easy one. "I'm supposed to be a gangster, right? For the party? You didn't have a tommy gun lying around, but I thought this would do."

She didn't look convinced, but she was trying. "You could always pretend to be Elliott Ness."

"Who's that?"

"Cut it out, Rafferty. I'm not interested in your little game. You know as well as I do that Elliott Ness is the man who finally put Capone in jail."

"Did he really? What did he manage to get him on? Murder? Racketeering? Bootlegging?"

"Tax evasion."

Rafferty just looked at her. "You're telling me the most notorious crook in the history of Chicago got sent up the river for a tax problem?" He was incredulous. "You've got to be kidding."

She no longer knew what to make of him, that much was clear. She simply shrugged. "Gospel truth," she said. "And I don't think you'd make it as a G-man. You're too haunted-looking."

"Good word for it," he muttered beneath his breath. He glanced at his watch, the kind that hadn't been made in more than fifty years. "It's getting close to witching hour. You sure you want to go to this party?"

"I promised." He was marginally pleased to realize she no longer thought it was such a good idea. "Besides, the two of us look perfect. It would be a waste if others couldn't appreciate us."

"A waste," Rafferty said. "You still want to wear that pillow coat? It doesn't really fit the dress."

"Pillow coat? You mean my down one?"

"I guess. Looks more like an oversize life preserver to me."

"I've got something better." She disappeared into her bedroom, then returned moments later with a fur coat over her arm. And it wasn't just any fur coat. It was the full-length silver fox Crystal Latour had conned out of Bugs Moran himself. Rafferty ought to know. He'd been the one to deliver it, some sixty-four years ago. And he'd been the one who'd been rewarded for it.

"So Crystal left you her fox, too?" he said, taking it from her and holding it out to her. The damned thing didn't feel any older than he did.

She glanced at him over her shoulder as she slid into it. She was thinner than Crystal, and taller, and the coat looked terrific on her. "How'd you know it was Crystal's?"

"You've got two choices. One, I saw her wear it some sixty years ago. Or two, it was a logical guess. Most states attorneys don't wear silver fox coats. Take your pick."

"Actually I don't like to wear fur. I hate to think of the poor little animals slaughtered for a woman's vanity. But since these particular animals were killed half a century ago I decided it would be okay."

"Yeah, you wouldn't want their sacrifice to be in vain," Rafferty drawled. He let his hands slide up the soft fur sleeves, and he could feel her tremble.

"Besides which, the coat was never worn."

That startled him enough to step back, reaching for his own wool overcoat. "Why not?"

"Crystal told me the man who delivered it was killed the next day, and she could never wear it without thinking of him. So she just put it in storage."

"Helluva waste of a thousand-dollar coat," Rafferty said.

"It would cost a lot more now."

"Then you'd better take good care of it, counselor. Make sure no one takes a tommy gun to you."

"Which reminds me. The gun you're carrying—it's not loaded, is it?"

"Trust me, Helen," Rafferty said, "nothing would happen if I fired it."

She wasn't going to be fobbed off with a half-truth. She stopped at the doorway, grabbing her oversize purse. "You didn't answer my question. Is it loaded?"

Push had come to shove. "I know how to use a gun, Helen. If I aimed it, cocked it and pulled the trigger, it wouldn't fire. Now there are three possible explanations for that. One, that it isn't loaded. Two, that the gun is broken, but you're the offspring of a family of cops, and you know enough about guns to keep yours in working order. The third possibility is that there is something to what I've been trying to tell you about who and what I am. Which will it be?"

For a moment she hesitated, and he could almost see what was going through her mind. He watched her warm brown eyes as once more she rejected the truth as too threatening. "The gun's not loaded," she said flatly. "Come on, Rafferty, if you're coming. And this time I get to drive."

Chapter Nine

Someone had done their research well. Rafferty walked into the cavernous garage and wanted to throw up.

The original garage on Clark Street had been a lot bigger, of course. It had been used to store bootleg liquor and getaway cars. There'd been no source of heat, either, and this place was warm enough for Helen to slip off Crystal's fox coat.

He didn't like the way the men looked at her. He'd never been particularly possessive—in his line of work it hadn't paid to be, and in the intervening years it would have been a waste of time. The garage was crowded, with men in pin-stripe suits and wide lapels, women in fringe laden chemises, and none of them looked quite right. They were all overgrown children, playing dress-up. All of them, that is, except Helen.

A group of men were playing cards at a table, and he felt a superstitious shiver run down his spine. He'd been one of the men playing that day. He could even remember the hand he'd held. A dead man's hand.

There was a crowded bar at one end of the brick garage, but most people seemed to be drinking coffee, which only made sense, given the early hour. He could see several elongated cigarette holders, and he reached for his own pack with a sigh of relief. Until he noticed that none of the other cigarettes were lit.

"Helen." The man who bore down on them wore spats, something that had gone out of style by the early twenties. "You look fabulous, darling, absolutely fabulous! And who have you brought with you?"

"This is a friend of mine. Jamey, this is Greg Turner, an old college friend. He's the man behind all this—his attention to detail is nothing short of phenomenal."

Rafferty could recognize the faintly veiled anxiety in Helen's voice. She wasn't any more enthralled with this tasteless party than he was, up to and including the men walking around with phony machine guns and brand-new fedoras. "It seems very accurate," Rafferty murmured, lighting his cigarette.

"Thanks, old man," Greg said. "I try to be. I'm afraid I'm going to have to ask you to put that out. This is a nonsmoking party."

Jamey just looked at him, imagining what any of his fellow victims of the infamous massacre would have said to such a stupid statement. As a matter of fact, he'd seen Ricky Drago respond to just such a request once, putting out his cigarette on someone's hand. For the first time he could understand the temptation.

He dropped the cigarette on the cement floor and ground it beneath his heel, not bothering to plaster a pleasant smile on his face. He didn't want to be here— the whole thing gave him the willies, but he wasn't about to leave Helen unprotected. Ricky Drago was a man who kept his word. He wasn't going to stop until he accomplished what he intended. Or until somebody stopped him.

Mary Moretti had picked a hell of a time to have a baby. Somehow Billy had to pull himself together and come up with a way to protect Helen, to stop Drago, by the time Rafferty left. And at this point, time was running out.

"Great suit," Greg continued, moving past Helen in a way Rafferty would have found completely nonsensical if he hadn't already recognized certain proclivities. "It really looks authentic. If I didn't know better, I'd say it really did come from the early thirties."

"Late twenties," Rafferty said.

"Oh, no, dear fellow. Trust me, this kind of suit wasn't made until 1932 at the earliest. I'm an expert on these matters," Greg announced.

This time Rafferty did smile. Greg took a sudden, nervous step backward, almost barreling into Helen. "I'm sure you're right," Rafferty said, having bought the suit in 1928 at a small tailor's shop not too many blocks away from this god-awful party. "Still, it's close enough."

"It's fabulous." Greg gushed, taking a step closer again. "How did you and Helen meet? She usually has such awful taste in men."

"Cut it out, Greg," Helen said in a calm voice. "Jamey doesn't need to hear about my love life."

"What love life, darling?" Greg responded. "What with that army of ogres you call your family, no man would dare get close to you. Except for your friend." Greg let his eyes wander over Rafferty. "You look like you'd dare just about anything."

"Just about," Rafferty said, moving past him and taking Helen's smooth bare arm in his hand, letting his touch linger possessively. "Let's get a drink."

She went with him docilely enough, which surprised him. "That was rude," she said in a breathless voice as he quick-stepped her over to the long table serving as a bar.

"Yes, it was," Rafferty said, reaching for a cup of coffee and handing it to her. He took his own and brought it to his lips, then stopped. "What the hell is this?" he demanded.

An older man was standing near them, and he turned and grimaced. "The worst Scotch money can buy," he said. "They're trying to duplicate bootleg liquor."

"Why in a teacup?"

"Because Greg is our host, and he's convinced everyone drank liquor out of teacups during prohibition," the man explained, taking a sip without shuddering.

"Not that I remember," Rafferty said dryly.

The man's eyes crinkled with amusement. "Me neither. But since none of us were born then, who's to know the difference? Hi, Helen."

"Hi, Mel. This is a friend of mine, Jamey...."

"Just Jamey," Rafferty interrupted, holding out his hand. Despite the occasional lapses, this was too well-informed a crowd to make free with his last name.

"Mel Amberson." The older man took it, giving it a decent shake. "You guys want to drink that swill, or do you want to know where they keep the good stuff?"

"Uh, Mel, it's a little early for liquor," Helen said, setting her untouched cup of whiskey back down on the table.

"No, babe, I'm talking about the really good stuff. Pure Colombian."

"Mel," Helen warned.

Mel grinned. "Coffee, honey. I'm talking about coffee."

"I'll be your slave for life," she said, casting a mischievous glance up at Rafferty. "Mel likes to tease me. He's known me since I was a baby, and he still thinks I'm wet behind the ears."

"To put it mildly. I was on the force with her old man. He and I were even partners for a couple of years, until I decided there were more honest ways to make a living."

"Mel's a stockbroker. A very successful one."

"That's just another word for professional gambler," Mel said. "The main trick is to earn money and keep a clean conscience."

Rafferty found he could laugh. "How do you manage to do that?"

"That's where I use my police background. I investigate. Find out who's dirty, who's clean. Who runs a tight shop, who rips off little old ladies, who screws up the environment, who has decent pensions and benefits. I find that the happier the workers, the stronger the company, and the stronger the company, the better the profits." He gave Rafferty a curious glance. "What do you do for a living, Jamey?"

"I'm retired," he said. "As a matter of fact, I used to be involved in gambling myself."

"Did you, now? How'd you do?"

Rafferty grinned, finally finding someone he liked. "Let's just say I had a certain gift for it." He hadn't even realized Helen had moved away until she reappeared, two mugs of coffee in hand. He took one, his fingers just brushing hers, and her eyes flew up to meet his for a brief, shaken moment before she stepped back.

"You say you're retired?" Mel said. "A young man like you? Ridiculous! If you ever need a job, look me up. I can always use someone with a certain gift. Picking the right stock isn't that much different from picking the right horse. You just have to have the talent."

For a moment it flashed before him, like a perfect jewel, just out of reach. The woman standing beside him, the scent of white roses mixing with the aroma of coffee. A job, a future, a life. And then it vanished like the pipe dream it was.

"I wish I could take you up on it," he said, not bothering to disguise his own regret. "But I can't stay."

"Says who?" Mel asked.

"He's been trying to convince me..." Helen began, and then her voice trailed off as he shot her a mild, warning look. "Been trying to convince me he'll settle down sooner or later," she continued smoothly. "But I'll believe it when I see it."

Mel nodded. "I can understand wanderlust," he said. "I had it myself. You two known each other long?"

"Long enough," Helen said, flashing her own warning look, and she threaded her arm through his.

"Your father met him? Or those brothers of yours?"

"Not yet," Rafferty drawled. "Should I be scared?"

Mel laughed. "If it were anybody else I'd say so. But you strike me as a man who can hold his own, even against five Chicago cops named Emerson."

"I imagine I can."

"Let me know if you change your mind," Mel said, clapping a hand on Rafferty's shoulder. "You got to settle down sooner or later, and I can always use a good man."

"That's the best offer I've had in a long time," he replied. "I wish I could say yes."

Mel looked between the two of them, and there was a very definite twinkle in his eyes. "I'm not sure if I believe *that*, son," he said. "But you keep me in mind if you ever need a job." A look of distaste crossed his face. "Lord, that little horror Greg is heading our way. I'm out of here, Helen. See ya."

"Let me walk you out," Rafferty said with a trace of desperation, but it was too late. Greg had already jumped in front of Mel, and beside him was a watered down version of Crystal Latour in her prime.

"This is Helen's friend," Greg gushed. "Have you ever seen anyone more marvelous?"

"Marvelous," the woman breathed. "Hi, Helen." She didn't even glance at Helen, her kohl-rimmed eyes glued to Rafferty.

"Hi, Clarissa," Helen muttered, and Rafferty could hear the annoyance in her voice. Clarissa had a quite spectacular body, one that usually would have interested Rafferty, but not today. Right now all he cared about was the slender, far more subtle woman beside him, not this brightly dressed creature looking him over as if he were a piece of blueberry pie.

Clarissa sidled up to him, and she smelled like Shalimar. He'd always hated Shalimar. "You look so realistic. Where did Helen find you?"

"He's a time traveler, Clarissa," Helen said irritably. "He actually comes from another century."

He looked at Helen and smiled. She was definitely annoyed with Clarissa. She was also undeniably jealous. It had been too long since he'd had time for someone to grow jealous over him. It felt good. It felt damned good. "I thought you decided it was just another planet," he said, and his eyes met hers in a rueful smile.

The tension was gone. "Mars," she agreed.

"Pluto," he corrected her, teasing.

"Well," Clarissa said, not one to be ignored, "you still look absolutely perfect for an occasion like today. You look just like one of those cold-blooded gangsters."

That artless statement drew his attention away from Helen. "I do? How would you define what they looked like?" he asked in a silken voice that should have warned the woman.

But Clarissa wasn't a sensitive soul. "Oh, you know what I mean. Ruthless. Sadistic. Amoral. Those men cared more about their clothes and their cars than they did about human life." Now that she'd got his full attention she was making the mistake of enjoying it. She tossed her mane of lacquered hair. "They were just a bunch of murdering hoodlums."

His smile was thin, threatening. "I don't think so."

Clarissa was still oblivious to his reaction. "I know what I'm talking about, Jamey," she insisted. "I've read..."

"The majority of men involved in the mob were family men," he said. "They earned money the only way they could to keep their families going during the Depression."

"Oh, grow up, Jamey!" Clarissa pleaded, almost getting her capped white teeth knocked down her throat for the trouble. "You've been seeing too many of Helen's old movies. No one believes that kind of romantic stuff about a bunch of cold-blooded killers anymore."

He wanted to refute her casual words. There were good, decent men, involved in not so good, not so decent work, and he wasn't that impressed with modern-day business in comparison. But the memory of Ricky Drago and his deadly usefulness wiped out any of Rafferty's possible defenses.

"Maybe you're right," he said instead, turning away from her.

She put her hand on his arm, possessively, and he was about to shake her off when he saw Helen's eyes narrow in rage. He left it there, enjoying the sensation of a woman caring enough to be angry. Angry enough to care.

"Where did you find this man, Helen?" Clarissa said again. "He's absolutely wonderful."

"He's mine," Helen said flatly.

Rafferty almost kissed her there and then. Instead he simply smiled, coolly, and detached Clarissa's clinging arm. "That I am," he agreed, and watched the blush rise to Helen's rouged cheeks.

Clarissa was a good sport. "Let me know if you get tired of him," she said, conceding defeat. "You know who you look like, Jamey? It's finally come to me."

"He looks like a cross between Humphrey Bogart and Cary Grant," Helen said sharply, and Rafferty almost expected to hear her say "he's mine" again.

"Perhaps," Clarissa conceded. "But he's a lot taller. No, he looks exactly like one of the guys in an old photograph I was looking at last night. A gangster."

Rafferty took a slow, careful sip of his coffee. It was already cold, and the noise from the party was overwhelming. He knew what was coming next. He just wondered how Helen was going to react.

She was still innocent. "It's the suit," she said.

"Uh-uh. It's the face," Clarissa said. "He's the spitting image of one of the guys killed in the massacre. One of Bugs Moran's more trusted lieutenants. What was his name? Doherty? Gogarty? Something Irish like that. I remember...Rafferty!"

Helen dropped her coffee. It landed at Clarissa's feet, shattering, splashing Clarissa's sturdy white legs. Rafferty moved Helen in time, protecting her white dress from the stuff. "You've got a good memory," he said evenly. He looked down at Helen, at her white face and huge, shocked eyes. "You ready to go, Helen?"

She could only nod. He took her arm and she followed, docilely enough, as he led her through the noisy crowd. "This party is awful," he muttered, reaching for her coat and draping it around her shoulders.

She stopped, staring up at him. "Did you tell her to say that?"

"Say what?"

"I didn't tell anyone your last name. You must have told Clarissa..."

"Helen, I haven't been away from your side in the last thirty hours. When would I have told her? Besides, she seemed too stupid to be able to carry something like that off."

"Clarissa is a circuit court judge," Helen said.

"You're kidding."

"Most of the people here are lawyers and judges. Rafferty..." Her voice trailed off, and she shook her head.

"Let's get out of here, Helen. I don't want to waste my last day in Chicago like this."

It didn't require much persuasion. "All right," she said, heading for the door.

There was something to be said for Greg after all. They were out the door, standing on the sidewalk, when their host came barreling after them, pushing between them in his effort to catch Rafferty's arm.

Helen slipped in her very high heels, falling sideways as the car roared around the corner. Rafferty heard the noise with a sickening sense of horror, and his next move was pure instinct, shoving Greg out of the way, diving on top of Helen as the thunderous sound of machine-gun fire filled the chilly February air.

And then suddenly all was a hushed, horrified silence. Until Greg pulled himself to his feet, shook himself off and announced, "God, that was absolutely fabulous!"

The door to the garage was full of guests, staring wide-eyed at the street, and an enthusiastic cheer went up. Rafferty's heart was still racing too fast to control, and beneath him Helen lay soft and panting, staring up at him with the same sort of panic he was feeling. And unless he was wrong, the same sort of desire.

And then hands hauled him upright, pulling Helen to her feet as well, as Greg continued to bounce over the sidewalk. "I can't thank you enough, Jamey!" he announced. "I never thought of staging a drive-by shooting. It was fabulous, just fabulous."

The idiot hadn't noticed the bullet holes in the outer wall of the garage, or seen the chips of flying debris. The whole gaggle of slightly tipsy legal minds thought Ricky Drago's latest attempt was nothing more than a party game. Rafferty wanted to knock some heads together.

He controlled the effort. Drago was long gone, but that didn't mean he wasn't crazy enough to turn around and try it again. The sooner they got out of there, the better.

Besides, Helen was swaying slightly on her feet, and her color wasn't that much better than the off-white velvet dress that fitted her slender body so perfectly.

"Let's go home, Helen," he said, shaking off Greg's enthusiastic embrace and putting an arm around Helen's shoulder. The fox coat had ripped in their fall, and for a moment he had the sudden terrifying thought that she might have been hit after all.

But she was tougher than he would have thought. "Yes, let's," she said in a slightly shaken voice.

"Home," Greg echoed archly. "Things have moved pretty quickly between you two."

"Try not to be too big a jerk, Greg," Mel said, stepping forward. His faded blue eyes surveyed them, and Rafferty knew that unlike the others, he hadn't missed a thing. "You need any help, Jamey?"

"We'll be fine."

Mel nodded, glancing at the bullet holes in Greg's brick garage. "The offer still holds, you know."

Rafferty managed a tight smile. "I only wish I could."

Helen was silent as he helped her into the car, silent when he leaned forward and fastened the seat belt around her. He was getting better with the stupid metal buckles, and Helen was in no shape to criticize. As a sop to her nerves he even fastened his own belt, as a sop to his own nerves he lit a cigarette, waiting to hear her start nagging. She said nothing as he pulled into traffic, barely missing an oncoming truck.

"Did you arrange that?" she asked finally, her voice slightly husky.

He glanced over at her. She'd managed to pull herself together, at least a bit, and he wondered how much he dared tell her. Whether she'd believe in Ricky Drago any more than she believed in him.

He shook his head. "It must have been someone else's clever idea. I wish to God they'd warned us. It scared the hell out of me. I thought those were real bullets."

He could see the tension in her shoulders relax slightly. "I almost thought so, too," she said. "It...it frightened me."

"Hell, it frightened me, too. I bet it was Greg's idea. He's enough of an idiot to think it might be entertaining."

"You're right," Helen said, breathing more evenly now. "A couple of years ago he had four men come in with machine guns loaded with blanks. Two men dressed as policemen and two in period clothes. We knew it was all part of the act, but when they pretended to fire on us it felt . . . real.''

Rafferty closed his eyes for a brief moment, then opened them in time to miss a fire hydrant. ''I know what you mean,'' he said roughly. He glanced out the rearview mirror, but there was no sign of Drago, at least for now. ''What the hell would you want to go to a party like that for? Apart from the sheer bad taste of it, they didn't seem like your kind of people.''

''And what are my kind of people?'' she asked, her voice cool and brisk. ''From our long-standing and intimate acquaintance I gather that you're more than ready to come up with a pronouncement. What kind of people do you think I belong with?''

''Not saps like them.''

''That's the problem, Rafferty. I don't know where I belong. I'm twenty-nine years old, and I've felt at home, really at home, with only a few people. My family, even though they drive me crazy. And as crazy as it sounds, Crystal Latour. I only knew her for a few short months, but we had a kind of understanding, a rapport, that you don't usually find. She told me I was born eighty years too late.''

Rafferty drove up over the curve, swore and pulled back into the street. ''She did, did she?''

Helen turned to look at him, and her brown eyes were very clear and certain. ''I feel at home with you, Rafferty,'' she said, her voice soft.

"Don't!" He pushed his foot down on the gas pedal, hard, but it was already floored. "I thought I warned you. I'm no good for you. Here today, gone tomorrow, and there's no way I can change it."

"Maybe it would be worth it," she said meditatively. "Maybe half a loaf is better than none."

Rafferty saw the outline of her apartment building with a sense of profound relief. He aimed the car for a narrow space near the front, zipped into it and slammed on the brakes.

Helen put out a hand to stop herself from hurtling toward the windshield. "Do you always have to drive like a maniac?" she asked mildly enough.

"Do you always have to behave like a maniac?" he countered. "I've warned you, and I'll warn you again. I'm no good. You can believe what you want, but even if you won't believe I'm a small-time gangster from sixty years ago, believe that I'm not the kind of man you want. I've lied to you..."

"If you were the Rafferty that died in the shoot-out then you weren't small-time," Helen pointed out, unfastening her seat belt.

Rafferty growled, "You're making me crazy."

Her smile was brilliant and absolutely devastating. "I'm doing my best."

He slammed out of the car, starting up the wide front steps. She caught up with him as he unlocked the door, putting her hand on his arm.

It was the last straw. He turned, to look down at her, at her wide, lost eyes, at her soft, vulnerable mouth, at the dress his own bride should have worn, and something inside him snapped. He'd stared death in the face too many times, not his own death, which no longer mattered, but hers. And suddenly he wanted to affirm life in the most basic possible way.

He pulled her into the hallway, slamming the door on the bright winter sunshine, cocooning them in warmth and darkness. Pushing her up against the wall, he slid his hands under the heavy fur coat, around her body and pulled her tight against him, against his own hard, aching body, wanting to scare her away, wanting to take her, wanting a thousand conflicting things.

She stared up at him, wordlessly. And since he made no move to kiss her, she reached up on her tiptoes and put her mouth against his, sweet and shy and very brave. "Come on, tiger," she whispered against his mouth. "What are you afraid of?"

"You, Helen. Just you."

Chapter Ten

Rafferty frightened her. There was no other word for it. As he stared down at her in the darkened hallway, his body pressed up tight against her, she could feel the tension, the need in his tall, wiry body. She could see the desperation and anger in his face. She was afraid of that intensity, that emotion. And the fact that she was mirroring those feelings.

But she was even more afraid of his leaving, disappearing, before she discovered just what it felt like. Afraid that once he was gone, as inevitably he would be, that she'd never experience those emotions again. And she was brave enough to take the risk.

"Rafferty," she said, but he put his hand over her mouth, his long fingers hard against her lips.

"Don't," he said, and there was no mistaking the desperation in his voice. "There's just so much I can take, Helen. I'm only human."

"I thought you were a ghost," she said, her voice deliberately taunting. "Or a zombie."

"Damn it." He moved his hand from her mouth, cupping the back of her neck beneath the heavy fall of hair and kissed her then, his mouth hard against hers.

She closed her eyes, sinking back against the wall, reveling in the feel of him, of his hard, taut body, of his hungry mouth, pushing her lips apart, tasting, devouring, as if a man obsessed. She wanted to kiss him back, but he was too forceful, allowing her no choice but to accept, passively, when she wanted more and more and more.

When he broke the kiss he was breathing heavily, and she could feel him against the soft cradle of her hips, feel how much he must want her. He couldn't turn her down this time, could he? She'd waited so long for someone she really wanted. She was tired of waiting.

"Helen," he said, his voice nothing more than a rasp of longing.

She cupped his face with her hands, his dear, tormented face. "I want you, Rafferty. I've been waiting all my life for you. Don't turn me away."

He groaned, sinking his head against the wall beside hers, and she could feel the shudder dance through his body, as he fought it, fought her, fought himself. And then with a muttered curse he dropped his hands to her shoulders, shoving the heavy fur coat off and onto the floor at their feet. He slid his fingers under the straps of the velvet dress and pulled them down, abruptly, baring her to the waist, and in the darkened hall she almost panicked.

"Trying to scare me off, Rafferty?" she whispered, stilling her reaction, keeping her hands from covering herself. "You can't do it."

"Can't I?" he muttered. And he pulled the dress down over her narrow hips, so that it fell at her ankles, and she was standing there in the hallway, dressed only in a pair of serviceable white cotton panties and white silk stockings rolled to her knees.

He scooped her up then, wrapping her around his body, her legs around his hips, her arms around his shoulders, pressing her against the wall as he kissed her again, his mouth hot and wet and seeking, his long fingers cupping her hips, squeezing, pressing her against him, and she could feel his heat and hardness at the very center of her.

She knew she should be frightened, and she was. She knew she should be turned off, and she wasn't. She wanted to feel his flesh against hers, his bare skin against her breasts. She wanted to lie on the big, empty bed in her room and have him show her what she'd been waiting twenty-nine years to discover. He was the right man in the right place at the right time, even if he didn't believe it.

She clutched him tightly, her fingers kneading his shoulders beneath the wool jacket. And then he broke the kiss, swinging her around dizzily, carrying her into the apartment, and she closed her eyes, expecting to see the bedroom.

Instead he dropped her on the couch, unceremoniously, making no move to follow her down onto the spacious cushions.

She was completely vulnerable, half-naked as she'd never been before with a man. She lay there, staring up at him, waiting.

He stood over her, his tie still in place, his face tense and dark, his breathing rapid. "This is no good, Helen," he said in a tight, angry voice. "You know it and I know it."

She didn't move. "You don't want me?" she asked in a forlorn voice.

He cursed then. Not a polite curse, not a gentlemanly curse, but with words that might have even shocked her hard-boiled brothers. "Damn it, Helen, don't you have any sense of self-preservation?" he said finally.

"Not where you're concerned. I'm in love with you."

The words horrified him almost as much as they shocked her. She hadn't realized it until she spoke it aloud, and the thought was astonishingly right.

"Helen, you don't know what you're talking about," he said, running a desperate hand through his hair. "You don't even know me."

There was a limit to her bravery after all, she discovered. A limit to how much she could offer, how much she could be rejected. Heat flushed through her body, and she struggled off the sofa as she tried to cover herself. "Sorry," she muttered in a miserable little voice. "I didn't mean to embarrass you."

He caught her as she tried to move past him, caught her in hard, strong hands. "I'm trying to do what's best for both of us," he said. "For once in my life I'm trying to do the right thing."

"Bully for you," she said, hating the burning of tears in her eyes. "Let me get some clothes on." She tried to pull away from him, furious now, furious and ashamed. She'd allowed her first real taste of passion to blind her, but now her eyes were opened, and she wanted nothing more than to hide. From him and from herself.

He didn't release her. A thousand emotions crossed his usually impassive face, and then he was very still, that threatening, enticing stillness. "I tried," he said, more to himself than to her, an excuse, an apology, a defiance. "Damn it, I tried." And he pulled her into his arms.

She fought him this time, pushing against him. "I've changed my mind," she said. "I don't want you after all."

"Fickle, aren't you?" he said wryly, kissing the side of her mouth, letting his lips trail down the line of her jaw, her throat, concentrating on the rapid pulse at the base of her neck. "I thought you were in love with me."

"What the hell do I know about love?" she said bitterly.

"Maybe I can teach you."

She stopped her struggles abruptly, standing very still. He released her, and she slowly brought her hands up to his tie. She unfastened it more deftly this time, even though her hands were trembling, even though she was doing her best to avoid his intent gaze.

She began to work on the pearl buttons of his white shirt, unfastening them slowly, one by one, until she reached the belt of his trousers. And then she leaned forward and put her mouth against his chest, against the hair-roughened flesh.

He sucked in his breath, and for a moment she wondered if she'd been too bold. And then his hands cupped her head, gently, as she tasted him, her tongue tracing tiny patterns on his flat stomach, as her hands reached for his thin leather belt.

He pulled her up then, into his arms, and somehow they made it over to the sofa as his mouth met hers. He pushed her back on the cushions, kneeling over her, still fully dressed, and his hands cupped her breasts, the first time she'd felt a man touch her, and his thumbs danced across the tight peaks, sending a shaft of desire streaking through her, arching her hips against his imprisoning legs. His mouth followed, wet and hungry, suckling her, and she moaned, a soft sound of pleasure and frustration.

They hadn't turned on any lights, and the February afternoon was gray and shadowed, but inside on the overstuffed old sofa there was heat and light, as Rafferty slid his hands underneath her panties and pulled them down, over her long legs, leaving the stockings in place.

She waited for him to strip off his own clothes, but he made no move to do so. Instead he lay beside her, pulling her against him, and her hands slid inside his open shirt, reveling in the heat and strength of his muscled flesh, as his mouth teased hers open, his tongue dipping, tasting, arousing. She could feel herself sinking into a swirling mass of sensations, existing in the delight of his mouth playing with hers, her breasts pressed up against his warm, hard chest, wanting nothing more in this life but his mouth, his mouth....

She jerked in shock as his hand reached between her legs, cupping her. For a moment she stilled, not sure if she was ready, but his mouth kept coaxing, distracting, as he gently, deftly stroked her.

"Open your legs, Helen," he whispered, moving his lips to trail a damp path along her cheekbones. "Come on, lady, don't be shy. Open them. It's not going to work with your knees together." There was just a trace of laughter in his voice, and she wasn't sure she liked it.

But she couldn't resist him. Not when his mouth was so enticing. Not when his hand was so deft. She relaxed, just slightly, and his fingers found her, sliding into the heat of her, moving with such instinctive wisdom that she whimpered.

"That's my girl," he whispered against her ear, nibbling on her earlobe. "Just relax, and you'll be fine. I won't hurt you, I promise."

A small part of her confused brain reminded her that it was supposed to hurt the first time. But she trusted him, believed him, as his fingers slid against her, deftly, insistently, and she was arching her hips against him, searching for something, she wasn't sure what, aching, longing, dying for him, as his tongue thrust deep into her mouth, his fingers thrust deep inside her, his thumb pressing, caressing, pushing, until suddenly she shattered, her body going rigid, as wave after wave of starshot darkness poured over her.

She was crying when it began to fade away. She felt foolish, but the tears kept flowing, and she buried her face against his shoulder, against the white shirt he still wore, and he cupped the back of her head, holding her there, soothing her in a strained voice as his other hand stroked the taut line of her back.

She could feel the tension thrumming through his body, the sheen of perspiration on his skin, the rapid pulse of his heart against hers. She wanted to look up at him, to kiss him again, to find out what would happen next, but she was afraid. Besides, his hands felt too good on her, stroking her, soothing her, calming her. He was the one who knew what he was doing, not she. She could relax, and trust him. She could melt against the safety of his strong, hard body and know he would take care of things. She could rest . . .

IT WAS A LONG TIME before Rafferty dared disentangle himself from her sleeping form. Lying there with her damp, exhausted, deliciously naked body pressed up against his had been its own sort of hell. If this endless, unreasonable cycle ever ended, if heaven and hell existed, he no longer had to fear where he'd end up. He just had a taste of the worst of it. And the best.

She murmured something when he pulled away from her, a soft sound of distress that tore at his heart. Maybe she really did love him. He hoped not. He wasn't worth loving. And there was nothing he could offer her, more than what he just gave her.

He draped the discarded afghan over her, but it didn't help. He still knew in intimate detail the shape of the body beneath it. Round where it ought to be round, narrow and delicate, damp and hot, she was absolutely perfect. And he didn't know if the iron hardness between his legs would ever go away, in this lifetime or any of the subsequent ones.

He'd done his good deed for the day, for the week, hell, for the whole century. He'd resisted everything she'd offered, giving, not taking. He'd tasted her, enough to know that she was everything he'd ever longed for, dreamed about, needed. He'd tasted her, treated her and left her intact, inviolate, still ready for the man who might deserve her.

He hated that mythical man. Hated him almost as much as he . . . cared for Helen. She deserved better than him, and he had made the supreme sacrifice for some ungrateful bastard who'd probably treat her like dirt. . . .

Whoa, Rafferty. Slow down. Helen was too smart to fall for a jerk, wasn't she? Except that she'd fallen for him, when she should have known better.

Maybe he should teach her a lesson. Maybe he shouldn't worry about breaking her heart—it would keep her from making the same mistake twice. Maybe he should strip off his clothes, pull back that afghan and finish what he'd started.

Then again, maybe not. He could always find justification for his most base desires. He'd come this far, resisted what he wanted most out of some noble whim. It would be stupid to blow it at this point.

He'd strip off his clothes all right. Take the coldest damned shower known to man, and if that didn't do it, he'd open all the windows and the let the freezing February wind try to cool his passion. After all, he wasn't going to worry about dying of pneumonia. That would be the easy way out, and he'd already learned that nothing was going to be easy for him.

He'd just spent the most erotic half hour of his life, and he hadn't even come. God help him, what would it have been like if he'd done what she wanted?

The bathroom smelled of white roses. He shrugged out of his jacket, staring at his reflection in the mirror. He looked like a different man, no longer cool and mocking. He looked like a man caught in a torment beyond his bearing. And before he realized what he was doing, he'd shoved his fist into the mirror, into his reflection, shattering the glass around his hand.

THE SOUND of the telephone woke her. The apartment was dark—a light snow was falling outside the window, and she was alone on the sofa, her grandmother's afghan wrapped around her.

She could hear the shower in the distance. Rolling on her back, she touched her body. A body that felt different, and yet not different enough. What had stopped him? Did he simply not want her enough? Was he angry that she'd fallen asleep?

The telephone was still ringing. She hadn't set the answering machine—she seldom did on the weekend.

Wrapping the cover around her, she struggled to her feet, catching the phone on its sixth ring.

"Want to find out about the man you're living with?" The voice at the other end responded to her husky greeting. "Want to find out about Billy Moretti?"

"Who is this?" she demanded sharply, her momentary fog vanishing.

"Want to find out who wants to hurt you, Ms. Emerson?" the damnably familiar voice said. "Don't trust Rafferty—he's a liar. Why do you think he hasn't left your side in the past twenty-four hours? He doesn't want you to find out the truth."

"The truth about what?"

"The answers to all your questions lie with me."

"Who is this?" she said again.

"Come and find out . . . 1322 Clark Street. I'll be waiting. But I won't wait long."

"But . . ."

"And come alone, Ms. Emerson. Rafferty wouldn't lift a finger to help you anyway, but I don't want him around. Come alone, and I'll tell you what you need to know. Unless you're willing to put your life in Rafferty's hands."

That was exactly what she'd been willing to do. The phone went dead before she could say so, and she stared at the receiver in blank dismay, as the confusing events of the past day and a half swept over her. Rafferty's sudden appearance in her life, an appearance that had started with a lie and never been explained satisfactorily.

The supposed near miss outside the courthouse, the stranger in the hospital, the phony drive-by shooting at Greg's that had left him white and shaken. What the hell was going on?

He wasn't going to give her answers, she knew that already. He'd just tell her more fairy tales. And while part of her wanted to pretend nothing had happened, that no one had called, the part of her brain that was sharp and legalistic wouldn't let it be.

She'd leave it up to fate. If Rafferty emerged from the shower before she'd dressed and left, then she'd confront him. Otherwise she'd find the answers to her questions at 1322 Clark Street.

Why did that address sound so familiar? It wasn't that far away, but it wasn't a section of town she was that familiar with. It was decent enough—middle class, filled with apartment houses and small businesses and retirement homes, and it was still daylight. She had more to fear from the unanswered questions in her own apartment than a stranger in a residential neighborhood.

He was still in the shower when she emerged from her bedroom, dressed in faded jeans and an old police academy sweatshirt she'd filched from her youngest brother. It had to be the longest shower known to man, and she was half surprised her meager hot water supply was still holding out. Unless he was taking a cold shower.

Rafferty and his showers were no immediate concern of hers, she reminded herself, trying to ignore the telltale throbbing in her heart, the tingling in her skin, the tenderness in her lips. When she saw him again she'd be better equipped to deal with him, to demand the truth from him. And maybe then she'd be able to accept the fact that he simply hadn't found her desirable enough to make love to.

She took her car keys from the floor where Rafferty had dropped them, pulled on the fox coat for lack of anything better to wear and headed out into the late-afternoon air. A light snow was falling, the sky was bleak and a strong wind was whipping down the street. Somewhere young lovers were getting ready to celebrate Valentine's Day. Somewhere people were eating candy and drinking champagne and flirting and kissing and planning futures.

Not for Helen. Not for today. She was going to end Valentine's Day just as virginal as the first one she celebrated. But at least she was going to have some answers.

It was getting dark when she finally found 1322 Clark Street. She'd made a half a dozen wrong turns, driven slowly on the slippery streets, unsure of her direction, so that by the time she pulled in across the street from the place, she was beginning to have her doubts about the wisdom of her choice.

The building was set back a ways from the neat sidewalk, with a wide expanse of stubbled, snow-covered lawn in front. She sat in the car for a moment, staring, as a woman walked down the street, two matched cocker spaniels at the end of a leash.

The dogs had been well behaved enough, trotting along, until they came up to 1322. Suddenly they jerked, one of them snapping at the leash, straining at it to get away from the property. The other one promptly sat back on his haunches and began to howl.

Helen had heard that sound before. The lonesome, eerie howling of a dog, and with sudden horror she remembered what 1322 Clark Street was: the original site of the garage where seven men had been gunned down so many years before.

Her hands were trembling as she tried to start the car again. In her panic she ground the gears, and the car stalled. She tried again, as the door opened, and a hand reached in and came down over hers.

"Running away, Ms. Emerson?" a soft voice asked.

His hand was painfully, sadistically hard on her wrist. She tried to peer out the door at the man standing there, but she couldn't see much beyond a pair of dark, half-crazed eyes and a wiry body.

"Let go of my hand," she said in a deceptively firm voice.

"I thought you came for answers."

"I changed my mind."

"You know where you are, don't you, Ms. Emerson?" the damnably familiar voice continued. It was someone she'd prosecuted, she knew it, but she couldn't place him. "Of course you do. Rafferty must have been more forthcoming than usual. But then, he couldn't be, even if he wanted to. He can't tell you about who and what he is. Who and what we all are. But he must have said something."

Irrational horror scampered down Helen's spine. She tried to jerk her hand away, but the fingers tightened, grinding her bones together so that she had to bite her lips to keep from crying out.

"Don't be scared of an address, Ms. Emerson," that evil, crooning voice continued. "A place can't hurt you. The old garage was torn down decades ago. Sure, the dogs won't go anywhere near the place, but other creatures aren't so sensitive. I thought this would be a fitting place."

"A fitting place for what?"

"For me to kill you. Sort of poetic justice, don't you think?" And the man knelt down beside her, and she found herself staring into a pair of mad eyes that had once looked sanely enough out of Willie Morris's face.

"Why would you want to kill me?" Her voice didn't even tremble. Even if her hands did.

Morris smiled, a sweet, eerie smile. "Let's just say I owe you." And he brought a gun up into her vision, a very small, very lethal-looking gun.

She was going to die. She accepted it calmly enough, having no other choice. This crazy man was going to shoot her, for no very good reason, and her fury at Rafferty grew. Damn it, she didn't want to die a virgin. She didn't want to die without having known love.

The irrational anger was so strong that she kicked out, slamming the door open and knocking Morris onto the sidewalk. She didn't need a second chance. She took off down the sidewalk, her fur coat flying after her, certain at any moment that a bullet would slam into her back. Morris didn't strike her as the sort of man who would miss a target, even one moving as quickly as she was.

She leapt across the street, directly into the woman with her two dogs. They went down in a tangle of howling and snapping, the leashes wrapping around the women, the dogs barking in fury as Helen tried to fight her way free, terrified that she was going to bring death to a stranger as well as to herself.

He came up behind her; she could feel his presence before his hands caught her, extricating her from the leather leashes, hauling her upright. She turned, cold and ready to face certain death. And instead she looked up into Rafferty's furious eyes.

"What the hell are you doing?" he demanded.

She stared at him mutely, ignoring the vociferous anger of the other woman as she tried to sort out herself and her dogs. Helen glanced around, but there was no sign of Morris, no sign of anyone at all besides the disgruntled dog walker, who gave her a look of fury before stalking down the sidewalk, her dogs still carefully skirting the boundaries of 1322 Clark Street.

Rafferty ignored them as well. "Are you going to answer me?" he asked in a tight voice. "Why did you sneak off without telling me where you were going? Why did you come down here, of all places?"

"I didn't know I needed to account to you for my actions. I didn't know I wasn't allowed out on my own," she shot back, irrationally angry now that the immediate danger was past.

"Damn it, Helen . . ."

"Stop saying 'damn it,'" she shot back. "You say it too damned much."

He caught her shoulders in his strong hands, and if they were hard on her skin, they were nowhere near as painful as Willie Morris's lethal grip. "Why are you here?"

"Willie Morris asked me to come down here. He said he had something to tell me. About you."

Rafferty said something a great deal more succinct than "damn it." "And you came? Without telling me?"

"I didn't know it was Morris. He didn't identify himself. And I didn't think I could trust you."

He looked as if he were doing everything humanly possible to keep his temper. Somehow his towering rage was reassuring. He wouldn't be that angry if he didn't care for her, at least a little.

"What did he want?" Rafferty demanded. "What did he tell you?"

She tried for a cool, disdainful smile, but it came out woefully lopsided. "I think you know as well as I do what he wanted," she said crossly. "He tried to kill me." And then, to her utter shame and amazement, she burst into tears.

Chapter Eleven

They drove back to Helen's building in silence. Rafferty paid less attention than usual to his admittedly erratic driving, but even a few near misses couldn't force a protest from Helen. She sat with the seat belt wrapped tightly around her, staring blankly out the window, the tracks of her dried tears on her pale face.

She probably got freckles in the summer, he thought irrelevantly. Not too many, just a smattering across her pert nose, maybe a dusting along her cheekbones. He'd never see her with freckles. He'd never feel the summer sun again. Funny, but up until this time he hadn't minded. But right now he minded like crazy. Not seeing Helen Emerson's freckles.

There was no sign of Drago following them, but he took a circuitous route just to be certain. By the time they reached Crystal's old house Helen looked as if she was on the ragged edge of control. And Rafferty knew he had no choice but to push her over, once they got inside. If he hoped to have any chance at all of saving her life.

She climbed out of the car before he had time to even turn off the key, running up the stairs and disappearing into the apartment. He half expected to find the door locked, but she'd left it ajar, and he closed it carefully behind him, using all three locks and the security bar as well. He didn't want to let Ricky Drago in without a sufficient amount of warning. And he didn't want to give Helen the chance to run off again, perhaps straight into another trap. He wasn't going to let her out of his sight until he had her safely delivered into the arms of someone who could protect her.

He found her in the kitchen, staring into the half-empty refrigerator as if she were looking for the meaning of life. "The cupboards are bare," Rafferty said, his deep voice startling in the quiet.

Helen still leaned on the refrigerator door. "I'm not hungry."

"If you're too hot we could always open a window," Rafferty drawled.

She slammed the door shut, turning on him, and he was glad to see that the frightened, listless expression had vanished, replaced by one of sheer wrath. "What the hell is going on?"

He held himself very still, watching her. It was amazing to him, his total inability to terrorize her. Most people had only to come face-to-face with his impassivity and they'd back down. Not Helen. She was tough in ways unimaginable for such a vulnerable woman. It was little wonder that he was undeniably obsessed with her.

"What do you mean?" He stalled.

"Who are you? Why have you moved in on me, so that I can barely go to the bathroom alone? I must have been stupid not to have noticed before, but Willie Morris very kindly pointed it out to me before he tried to kill me," she said, her voice acid. "Who are you, who is Billy Moretti, who is Willie Morris? Do you all want to kill me? What in God's name is going on here?"

Her voice was rising in agitation. She heard it as well as he did, and with a great effort she took a deep breath, calming herself. "I want you to tell me the truth, Rafferty. No more science fiction stories, no more time travel, no more fairy tales. Just the plain, unvarnished truth."

"I told you . . ."

"I know what you told me. You're a dead gangster from 1929, and so was Billy Moretti. Perfectly believable," she snapped, and he could see the edge of panic dart behind her warm brown eyes. "So how does Willie Morris fit into all this? Who was he, Elliot Ness?"

"That's the second time you've mentioned Elliot Ness, Helen, and I don't have the faintest idea who you're talking about," Rafferty said wearily.

"Stop it!" Her voice broke, and she turned away. "I want to know what you're doing here, and what you want from me. Are you going to kill me?"

He wanted to touch her. He wanted to reach out and clasp her shoulders, pull her back against his strong body and warm her, soothe her, protect her. He clenched his fists to keep them at his side.

"If I wanted to kill you I've already had a dozen chances," he said. "I'm trying to protect you."

She turned back. "Why?"

"Ricky Drago plans to kill you. I'm doing my damnedest to stop him."

"Who the hell is Ricky Drago? And where does Willie Morris come into this?" she asked fiercely.

He'd forgotten Drago's new identity. "Drago and Morris are the same man," he said, trying to come up with something believable for a woman who didn't want to believe. "I knew him a long time ago... you might say in another lifetime."

"Why does he want to kill me? And why do you want to save me?"

"He blames you for his wife's death."

"What?"

Rafferty shrugged. "Don't expect me to understand. I wasn't even around when it happened. Apparently you brought him in for questioning, and he was in such a rage about it he drove into a cement bridge. He wasn't hurt but his wife was killed."

"God, I remember," she said, some of her ferocity fading. "But that was almost two years ago. Why would he want to come after me now?"

"Drago... er... Morris is a very methodical, very meticulous man. He never forgets a grudge, and he's not quite sane. Knowing him, I expect he always planned to get around to you in his own good time. And that time is now."

"Why you?"

He reached for his cigarettes. "What do you mean?"

"Who appointed you Sir Galahad, to come to my rescue like a knight in shining armor? Why do you care whether I live or die?"

He toyed with a dozen answers, some of them plausible, some of them truthful. He went for the most painful. "It was a favor to Billy."

He might as well have slapped her. Her face turned even paler, and she leaned against the refrigerator to steady herself. "Why does it matter to Billy?"

"He figures he owes you. You were right about him—he's trying his damnedest to go straight. Drago decided to put a monkey wrench in the works, and it was simple enough to get Billy to play along. All he had to do was threaten his wife. You had the wisdom to see that Billy was worth another chance, and he's not going to stand by and let Drago gun you down."

"And if it weren't for the baby's unexpected appearance he would have been the one in my apartment?" she asked, tossing back her long dark hair.

"Until he found someone to protect you," Rafferty agreed. His cigarette tasted foul, almost as foul as his temper. She was looking at him like a whipped dog, still ready to bite, and he knew he needed to demoralize her further.

"But he did, Rafferty. He found you."

"I'm only a stopgap. I'll be gone by tomorrow morning, and there won't be anyone between you and Drago."

She took a deep breath, her eyes meeting his. "That'll be just too bad, won't it?" she said.

"You come from a family of cops, Helen. I want you to call up one of your brothers and go stay with him until Billy can figure out what to do."

"No."

He stared at her incredulously. "A man tried to kill you," he said, biting off the words. "It wasn't the first time. Did you get a close look at the fur coat? There are bullet holes in it. Drago wants you dead, and he's not going to stop until he accomplishes that goal. Or until someone stops him."

"That's what you're here for, right? As long as the ghost of Valentine's Past is around, how can he hurt me?"

"Damn it, Helen!" He slammed his fist against the refrigerator, not even flinching as the force of his blow reopened some of the tiny cuts on his lacerated hand. "I can't save you!"

"Why not?" she demanded coolly. "Don't you have superpowers, or something like that?"

"Hell, I don't have any powers whatsoever," he snapped. "I can't shoot Drago. As long as I'm living in limbo I can't harm another living being."

"Guess what, Rafferty," Helen said softly. "You already have." She pushed past him, walking out of the kitchen, and for a moment he stood there, absorbing the force of her verbal blow.

She was standing in the living room, staring out into the snowy evening, her back straight and narrow beneath the baggy sweatshirt. Rafferty had never understood modern women's predilection for baggy men's clothes, but at that moment he couldn't imagine anything more desirable than Helen Emerson.

"I can't save you, Helen," he said again, more quietly. "And I don't want to watch you die."

She didn't turn. "Cheer up, Rafferty. You'll be back in limbo by the time Drago or Morris or whoever he is gets to me."

"You don't believe me."

"I don't know what to think. If you expect to convince me you're a bootlegger who returns from the dead every Valentine's Day then you're expecting a lot."

"Call your family. I'll drive you there."

She laughed then, but the sound was almost without humor. "I thought you wanted to save my life, not kill me. Your driving is the closest to death I've come in years."

"Helen . . ."

"Don't worry about it, Rafferty. I won't make any more demands on you." She turned and sank into the corner of the sofa, staring at her knees. "You should have made it clear sooner that you were here under duress. I suppose it was only logical to pretend you were attracted to me in order to keep an eye on me, but really, you should have told me the truth. I'm a big girl, I can take it. I would have called the State's Attorney and—" She halted. "I don't know what I would have told him."

"Stop it, Helen."

She shrugged, and he could see the effort it was taking, to appear cool and collected. He despised himself, more than he ever had hated himself before, and he didn't know what to do. He wanted to soothe her, to comfort her, to kiss her, to make love to her, and yet any act of kindness, or desire, would be the worst possible thing he could do.

"He probably wouldn't have believed me," she said in a low voice. "I don't believe it, either. You know, Rafferty, I think you'd better leave. You don't want to be here, and if you have to leave Chicago by tomorrow morning I imagine you have better things to do than baby-sit me."

"There's only one thing I hate more than baby-sitting," Rafferty snapped. "And that's self-pity."

"Go away, Rafferty. You've made it more than clear you don't want me. Let me sulk in peace."

"The hell I will!" It was the last straw. He'd wasted almost his entire stay, blown it on an impractical, self-centered, abysmally untried *girl,* and now she was sitting there feeling sorry for herself. He was the one who'd been suffering, and all for the most noble of reasons. Suddenly he'd had enough.

He crossed the room, reached down and hauled her to her feet. She was so startled she tripped against the coffee table, falling against him, which suited him just fine. "I'm sick of this," he said in a furious voice. "I've been going through the most miserable time of my life, all in some stupid, misguided effort to spare you, and all you can think about is that I don't want you. How damned stupid can you be? What do you think this is?'' He took her hand, yanked it down and pressed it to his groin.

She tried to jerk away, but he wouldn't let her. ''I've been going crazy, trying to do the decent thing,'' he went on, his voice bitter. ''I'm trying to save your life, I'm trying to leave you in the state I found you, no matter how damned much it's killing me. I want you more than I've ever wanted a woman in my life, but I don't want you wasting your innocence on a man like me, a man who can't offer you anything more than a night.''

For a moment she didn't move. ''Maybe a night is worth it,'' she said in a rough voice. And her fingers pressed against him.

He shuddered. ''Damn it, Helen.''

''Stop saying damn it,'' she said, ''and kiss me.''

He couldn't, wouldn't fight it any longer. When he finally emerged from the bathroom earlier that afternoon, marginally cooled down, his lacerated hand roughly bandaged, only to find her missing, panic had swept through him. He'd raced out into the street after her, just in time to see her taking off into the darkening afternoon, and it had been sheer instinct that had led him to Clark Street. Instinct, and a car it had taken him approximately four minutes to hot-wire and steal. There were certain talents that never grew rusty, even after sixty-four years.

He'd seen Drago from a distance, and he'd learned one thing. He might not be able to pull a trigger, but he could slam a car into another one. Drago had been knocked to the ground, his gun went flying and by the time Rafferty had disentangled Helen from the furious dog owner he'd taken off. And Rafferty's hands hadn't stopped shaking until he'd gotten her back to the apartment.

They were shaking again, this time with longing. He was going to take her, and to hell with scruples, and her future, deserving husband. To hell with everything but the need that had been burning a hole inside him.

"Sir Galahad, eh?" he said, scooping her up into his arms, holding her high against his chest. "Knight in shining armor?" He started through the apartment, kicking open the door to her bedroom. The sight of that unmade, pristine white bed made him harder than ever, something he wouldn't have thought possible.

He set her down on the rumpled sheets, disentangling her clinging arms as he stood back to watch her. And then he began stripping off his tie, kicking off his shoes.

She didn't move, her eyes wide and still in the shadows. "What happened to your hand?"

"It collided with your bathroom mirror." He stripped off his jacket and shirt, tossing them onto a chair. "It's better known as acute sexual frustration."

"You really want me?" The notion still seemed to amaze her, and he wondered what she'd gone through in her life, to be so unsure of her powerful attractions.

"I'm about to demonstrate just how much," he said, reaching for his belt buckle.

She closed her eyes when he shucked off his trousers, and he almost called her bluff. But he didn't. Instead he climbed onto the bed, taking her face between his hands, gently, and kissed her lips. Slowly, delicately, tasting the softness, the tremulous dampness, as her eyes opened in the darkness. "You can change your mind," he said in a soft voice. "Anytime you want, I won't force you."

"You don't want me that much?"

"Damn it," he said, and then managed a wry smile. "Okay, no more damn its. I want you. I thought I made it clear how much. But there's one thing more important than how much I want you. And that's you."

"Rafferty, I love..." she said, but he covered her mouth with his long fingers, afraid to hear the words again. The more she said it, the more real it became. And he couldn't afford to believe she loved him. It would make it too hard to leave.

So he simply kissed her again, teasing her mouth open, using his tongue, feeling the tremulous response as he deepened it. He kissed her with slow, deliberate thoroughness, leaving no part of her lips, her mouth, her teeth untouched, kissed her until she couldn't breathe, he couldn't breathe, and neither of them cared.

The baggy sweatshirt came off easily enough, followed by the thin scrap of bra. That was one improvement in modern times—underwear was far less cumbersome and a great deal easier to dispose of. The same for clothes in general, even though he felt damned funny unfastening the pair of men's jeans she wore. But there was nothing masculine about the pristine white cotton panties, nothing masculine about the soft mound of flesh that he put his hand on, feeling her arch against him.

His mouth left hers, to trace a path down her body. He wanted to kiss her breasts again. How could he have ever thought they were too small? They were perfect, in his hands, in his mouth, and he let his tongue swirl around each small, tight nub, reveling in the shiver of reaction in her slender body, reveling in his own fierce pleasure.

Her stomach was flat, white and smooth. He kissed her navel, he kissed her hips, he kissed the white cotton covered core of her. He kissed her long thighs, that writhed beneath him, he kissed her knees and her calves, he kissed the delicate arch of her feet.

"Rafferty," she said, and her voice was strangled, distorted with need.

"Not yet." He slid his long fingers underneath the panties and pulled them down her legs, tossing them across the room so that she lay there, naked, aroused and frightened. He didn't want to scare her further, but he already knew what he wanted, and nothing short of mass hysteria could stop him.

He leaned forward and put his mouth on her. She jerked, and he heard her quiet little shriek of shock and protest, but he ignored her, cupping her hips with his big hands, spreading her legs, kissing her, tasting her, loving her, ignoring her shock and shyness and uncertainty, ignoring everything but the flowing response he was eliciting, a response that flowered and built, as her hands dug into his shoulders, her heels dug into the mattress, and her whole body convulsed against him.

She was shivering, sobbing, gasping for breath, but he wasn't finished with her. He knew how to prolong it for her, how to make her cry out in the darkness, and he did so, drinking in her pleasure with such intensity that he almost came, too.

"Jamey," she said, her voice raw and weak. His mouth left her, and he moved up her body, to lie on top of her, careful not to crush her, his desperate, massive hardness in the cradle of her thighs as his hands framed her shocked face.

He kissed her lips, knowing she could taste herself on his mouth. He kissed her eyelids, her throat, tasting the rapid, erratic pulse beneath his tongue, as he spread her legs apart beneath him. She was still too weak and trembling from the aftermath of her climax to help him, but he didn't mind. He needed all his strength to control himself, to control his mindless need to surge into her damp heat, to push and thrust and burst.

He could feel the sweat cover him as he poised himself at the untried entrance. His muscles were clamped with the effort to slow himself, control himself, as he began to push inside. She was wet, and sleek, and very tight, and her eyes flew open, meeting his as he reached the inevitable barrier.

Rafferty thought he might just possibly die. It was too hard, too good, and he didn't know if he could stand it. He looked down at her, the flowing veil of hair spread out around the white pillow, the wide dark eyes, the soft bee-stung lips, and he pressed, slowly, feeling her pain, feeling her pleasure.

"Don't stop," she whispered, and her hands were digging into the sheet. "Please, Jamey, don't stop."

"I couldn't," he said simply. And with a short, sharp thrust of his hips he broke through, sinking fully into her tight, milking warmth.

Her arms came around him, holding tight, and he could feel the tremors rocketing through her body, and he didn't know if they were tremors of pain or desire.

He tried to pull away, but her arms were tight around him, holding him against her. He reached up and cupped her face, his thumbs gentle on the soft planes. "This doesn't work if we don't move," he whispered.

She opened her eyes. "I know," she whispered back. "I've read books."

"Naughty girl. Did I hurt you?"

"Not much." It was a lie, he knew it, but only a little one.

"I'll make it feel better," he promised, pulling away from her, just slightly, and then thrusting back in. She lay passively enough beneath him, and he let her, doing all the work, content to prolong it, intent on taking every last ounce of delayed pleasure from her, as her hands dug into his shoulders, her hips began to meet his measured thrusts, and he could feel the tremors of response begin to ripple and build within her.

He wanted, needed to come in her lithe young body so badly he was shaking with it. But he needed her there, too, more. It didn't matter that he'd already given her pleasure, it didn't matter that he deserved his own. He couldn't find it without her, and even as he felt his body shake apart he knew he had to bring her with him.

Her fingernails dug into his shoulders. Her hips arched beneath him, milking him, calling to him, and her breath was sobbing in his ear. Even through the swirling mists of his own fierce need he could taste and feel the nuances of her response, could feel her balance at the very precipice, ready, trembling, terrified.

He put his hand between their bodies, touching her, as he surged into her, pushing her hard against the soft white mattress. He felt her explode around him, gripping him with a thousand tiny tremors, and he lost himself, filling her with his body, his soul, drowning them both in a vast storm of helpless, hopeless love.

He knew he was heavy, but he didn't want to get off her. He cradled her head in his arms, kissing the dampness from her face as his breathing slowly returned to normal. He wanted her arms and her legs wrapped around him, tightly. Maybe if they just stayed this way he wouldn't have to leave her.

But he was a man who faced the unpleasant things in life, and clinging to Helen wouldn't keep him here, and it wouldn't keep her safe. He moved to one side, pulling her with him, wrapping her around him, and she came willingly, burying her head against his shoulder, her face hidden against his skin. He stroked her hair, gently, soothing her, listening to her shuddering breathing slow, listening to her thudding heart as it regained a normal rhythm. He waited until he thought she was ready, and then very carefully tilted her face up to his.

She didn't want to meet his gaze, and he realized with heartbreaking amusement that she was shy. "How are you feeling?" he asked softly.

Even in the darkness of the bedroom he could see the blush that covered her face, and he wished he had enough time to spend with her to show her enough that she was well past blushing. But that would be up to someone else. "Okay," she said.

"Okay," he echoed, not bothering to disguise his amusement. "That's not much of a recommendation. Was it worth the wait?"

Her eyes flew up to meet his then, and there was such deep emotion in them that he almost wished she were still shy. "Don't you know?" she asked.

The humor fled. "I know," he said, brushing his lips against her, running his tongue over her swollen mouth. "I didn't want to hurt you."

"You didn't. Not much," she added with characteristic honesty.

He kissed her then, a brief, hard kiss, before he pulled away from her, climbing off the high white bed. She watched him leave, not saying a word, and a moment later he was back with a cool, wet washcloth.

"What are you doing?" she demanded warily, her defenses already returning.

He pushed her gently down on the bed. "Taking care of you," he said, pressing the cool cloth against her. She jerked against the touch of the cloth, the touch of his hands, but she quieted immediately, watching him out of dark, wondering eyes.

"You didn't use anything," she said after a moment.

"Use anything?"

"Protection," she said, her voice low. "A condom. I should have thought..."

"It's okay."

"Okay for you, maybe."

He pushed her hair out of her face. "Okay for you," he said gently. "You won't get pregnant. You won't get any diseases."

"What makes you so certain?" she asked in a disgruntled tone of voice, pushing her face against his hand like a kitten searching for affection.

For a moment he said nothing. He didn't want to argue anymore, or try to convince her. He hadn't wanted to make love to her for any number of reasons. He hadn't wanted to steal her virginity from some man who'd treasure it and deserve it, though God knows no man could treasure it more than he had. He hadn't wanted to love her, knowing he would have to abandon her without warning. And he hadn't wanted to get so close, knowing that he was, in effect, living a lie, simply because the truth was so unbelievable.

"I can't harm you," he said wearily, knowing she wouldn't believe him. "No pregnancies, no diseases."

"Does my virginity magically return as well?" she asked tartly.

He found he could smile. "Counselor, I wish I could say you'd be the death of me, but it's already too late for that."

"You aren't going to tell me the truth, are you?"

"You aren't going to believe the truth," he replied. He reached for his shorts, pulling them on with a spare movement, both to protect her uneasy modesty and to try to control his still lively reaction to her.

It was a mistake. She stared at him, her eyes wide with sudden shock. "What are you wearing?"

He looked down. They were common enough, baggy white linen shorts that came almost to his knees. He had his custom-made in Ireland, with a row of tiny pearl buttons he was in the midst of fastening. He smiled wryly. "Men's underwear. Made in 1929. They've worn well, haven't they?"

"Rafferty . . ."

He wasn't in the mood to argue. "Why don't you take a long hot bath? I'll see if I can find something for us to eat in your empty icebox."

"It's not an icebox," she said mutinously, her dark eyes anxious, and he wished she hadn't been a virgin and didn't need time to recover, wished he could push her back down on the bed and start all over again.

He had to content himself with pressing his mouth against the corner of her eye, feeling her arch up against him, feeling her hands reach for him. "It is to me," he said. "And you're a mouthy dame." He kissed her lips, for good measure, before he headed for the bedroom door.

"I just wish I knew what you were, Rafferty," she said, her voice forlorn. And he closed the door behind him, trying to shut out temptation.

Chapter Twelve

By the time Helen emerged from the bathroom Rafferty had heated two cans of soup, eating one of them, made six pieces of toast and butter, and smoked three cigarettes. He sat at the café table in the corner of the kitchen, drumming his fingers on the plastic tabletop, his nerves on edge. He would have thought that finally making love to the recalcitrant Ms. Emerson would have taken some of the tension away. Instead, it only seemed to build.

He'd washed the dishes, more out of boredom than a need for order. He'd called Billy, only to find he'd already headed over to the hospital for nighttime visiting hours. He considered calling Helen's family, then thought better of it. If he called, she'd be out of his hands, no longer his responsibility. He'd have maybe another six hours to enjoy himself.

But the fact of the matter was, he didn't want to waste even five minutes of his remaining time away from Helen—not if he could help it. And he wasn't ready to trust anyone, even Helen's own family of police, to protect her from someone as devious and murderous as Ricky Drago.

He had to take care of Drago himself. He had no idea how he was going to manage it—although he still carried Helen's loaded gun, he'd already ascertained that the weapon simply refused to work in his hands. That didn't mean he couldn't lure Drago into doing something to himself. The details were sketchy, but Rafferty's determination was very clear. He alone could stop Drago. And he had to make sure Helen was safe while he did it.

She looked scrubbed, pink cheeked and shy when she finally walked into the kitchen. She was wearing men's clothes again, a black T-shirt that clung to her subtle curves, faded jeans that hugged her long legs. She'd pulled her brown hair behind her in a ponytail, probably trying to look businesslike. She only looked more luscious.

"There's soup and toast," Rafferty said, stubbing out his cigarette. "And coffee. Unless you'd rather get something at the hospital."

She'd been carefully avoiding his gaze. "The hospital?" she said pouring tomato soup into a mug and bringing it over to the table.

"I thought you wanted to visit Mary and Billy."

"I forgot."

"Well," Rafferty drawled, "things have been distracting the past twenty-four hours."

She looked at him then, and he wanted to kiss the faint stain of color from her cheekbones. "I'd like to see the baby," she said.

"Eat your soup first."

"Are you going to leave me there?"

He stalled for time, reaching for his cup of black coffee and taking a sip. She could see through him, much too clearly. After tailing her for the past thirty-six hours, how could she know he was planning to pass her on to Billy while he went after Drago himself?

"Why do you ask?"

"I know you."

"You've known me less than two days. That makes you an expert?" He kept his voice cool and mocking, the same tone he used to put pushy women in their place.

It didn't work with Ms. Emerson. "Yes," she said. "Are you going to answer me?"

"I've been beside you almost every moment since Billy told me you had a problem. Why should things change at this point?" He reached for his pack of cigarettes. One crumpled, one left. He put it back in his breast pocket with a sigh.

"I don't know, Rafferty. I just have a bad feeling about this."

"I'm not going to let Drago hurt you," he said. "No matter what I have to do, I won't let him get to you. I'll protect you from the bad guys."

"But Rafferty," she said patiently, "who's going to protect me from you?"

And to that he had no answer at all.

SHE LET HIM DRIVE to the hospital. By this time she'd grown inured to the headlong speed with which he drove, and even if her pretty little Toyota was accumulating more than its share of scratches and dings, at least she'd have something to remember him by when he disappeared.

She had no doubt whatsoever that he would be gone by tomorrow morning. She just didn't believe in his stated destination. People didn't return from the dead, year after year after year. And if they did, they weren't gorgeous-looking gangsters who walked into a virginal state's attorney's life and proceeded to turn it upside down.

Jamey Rafferty was just a man, either a crazy man, or a man with a twisted sense of humor. Although neither of those explanations rang true, the alternative was far too bizarre. She wasn't going to ask any more questions, especially since she couldn't believe the answers. She was simply going to take what was given her, up to and including every spare minute she had with Rafferty. Tomorrow would be soon enough for reality to intrude.

There was no sign of that mysterious black sedan following them into the hospital parking lot. She had no doubt whatsoever that Morris, or Drago, or whatever his name was, wanted to kill her. She'd looked into those mad eyes, into the barrel of that lethal-looking gun, and known death.

She had no doubt that Billy had asked Rafferty to watch over her, or that Rafferty had taken on that task unwillingly. And she knew that by tomorrow morning, Rafferty would be gone.

She ought to call her family—if she had any sense of self-preservation that was exactly what she'd do. If she called her boss she'd have to come up with proof. If she called her father or brothers she'd have to listen to endless lectures, questions, demands about her personal life, and they'd forcibly remove Jamey Rafferty from her life before she even had a chance to say goodbye.

Tomorrow was soon enough for that. When she woke up, alone, she'd reach for the phone and call her older brother Eddie. He'd be at her house with a cruiser and an armed guard within minutes. If Drago-Morris thought he could take on the assembled might of the Emerson branch of the Chicago police department he was in for a rude awakening.

Until then, she'd take her chances with Rafferty. Because something told her that once he left, he'd be gone for good. And she needed to hoard and treasure every second she had left with him.

Maternity was on the fifth floor. Rafferty put his hand on the small of her back as they entered the elevator, and she told herself the gesture was a protective one, not a romantic one. And still her skin tingled beneath the warmth of his flesh.

"I thought only family was allowed," she whispered to Rafferty as he moved her along the busy corridor, past eagle-eyed nurses and dewy-eyed new parents.

"I told them you were Billy's sister."

"And what does that make you?"

"Your husband."

She wanted to hit him. She never would have guessed she'd have such an intense reaction to the thought, but it felt like a blow to her stomach. She wanted him to be her husband. She wanted to carry the baby he said was impossible. She wanted everything from him, but most especially she wanted all his tomorrows. And she wasn't going to get even one more valentine.

The hospital room was filled with flowers. Billy was sitting in a chair, holding his baby son, while Mary watched fondly. Some of the warmth in her expression faded into anxiety as she spotted Rafferty, but she managed to smile anyway. "We weren't sure if you could make it tonight," she greeted them softly.

"I wouldn't have missed it for the world," Helen said, skirting the bed, leaving Rafferty in the doorway as she peered over at the tiny, red-faced newborn.

"Thanks for the flowers, Rafferty," Mary said in her shy little voice. "They're very pretty."

Helen threw a curious glance over her shoulder at Rafferty, standing still and silent. He must have called in an order for the bouquet, which was an obvious gesture, but if Rafferty was who he'd said he was, mastering the art of phoning in flowers and using credit would be beyond him.

Who was she fooling? Of course he wasn't who he said he was. He was just a man. An extraordinary man. A man she was fool enough to be in love with. But a man.

"Can I hold the baby?" she asked Billy.

Billy glanced over at Mary, who nodded permission. He placed him in Helen's arms with a sure touch astonishing in so new a father, and as Helen settled into the chair he'd just vacated, the baby snuffled, shoving a tiny fist into his mouth.

"He's absolutely gorgeous," Helen whispered, as a wave of longing swept over her. Rafferty had lied about so many things. Perhaps, if she were really lucky, he might have lied about the possibility of her getting pregnant.

"I need to talk to you, Billy," Rafferty said, still standing by the door.

"What about?" It was Mary's question, her voice disturbed.

"Don't worry, Mary, I'm not taking him anywhere. We'll be right outside the door for a few moments."

Helen watched as Mary schooled her emotions, managing a tight smile. The door swung silently shut behind them, and Mary leaned back against the stack of pillows.

"I know I'm being silly," Mary said in a weepy tone of voice.

"It's hormones," Helen said pragmatically, gently stroking the baby's tiny hand.

"So they tell me. I think I'd be happier if I were home, but Billy has this bee in his bonnet. If it were up to him, I'd be here on my back for a full two weeks just as the women of his mother's generation."

Helen looked down at the baby's sleeping face as Mary's words penetrated, and a disbelieving panic swept over her. "Billy would have been born in the sixties," she said carefully. "Women didn't spend more than a few days in the hospital back then."

Mary's face turned pale. "Of course. I don't know what I was talking about," she said nervously, guiltily. "And besides, I ought to be grateful I have a few extra days of rest. I certainly could use it. Labor wasn't that long, but it's exhausting, and I—"

"He *was* born in the 1960s, wasn't he?" Helen broke through Mary's babbling.

There was dead silence in the room, broken only by the even, snuffling sound of baby Jamey's breathing, as Mary stared at her. "I can't believe he told you," she said finally. "Billy said Rafferty had never told a living soul...."

"Told me what, Mary?"

Mary let out a nervous little moan, clapping her hands over her mouth. "Nothing."

"You don't believe that story, do you?" Helen persevered, trying to hold on to her own sanity. "Did Billy tell you the same pack of lies, about being from the 1920s? You can't have believed it!"

"He didn't...I mean, I don't..." Her voice trailed off, as her big eyes filled with tears. "I don't want to talk about it."

Helen stared at her, torn by guilt and exasperation and a very small trickle of fear. How could Mary have swallowed such a pack of lies? They had to be lies, didn't they?

The door opened, and Billy breezed back in, a calm, affable expression on his face that Helen didn't believe for a moment. There was no sign of Rafferty.

"Let me take this little bundle of joy from you, Ms. Emerson," he said, scooping the tiny infant from Helen's gentle hands. "Kind of makes you think about starting a family yourself, doesn't it?" he said cheerfully. "Nothing like a baby to make a man realize what matters in this life."

"Where's Rafferty?"

"He had to check on a few things," Billy said easily. "He said you had a little trouble with Willie Morris. I'm sorry about that—I should have warned you, but I didn't know quite how dangerous he was. And I was a little worried about Mary and the baby. I have to thank you again for dropping the charges. I don't know what I would have done if Mary had gone into labor and I'd been stuck in Joliet."

Helen watched as he tucked the baby back into the little bassinet. "Why don't you tell me your version of the past," she said evenly. "I've already heard Rafferty's spin on things."

He looked just as shocked as Mary had. "Rafferty told you?" he echoed.

"Of course I didn't believe him. I'm not as gullible as I look."

"Of course," Billy said vaguely, obviously trying to get his bearings. "That Rafferty's a great kidder. I always told him he should've been a writer. For Buck Rogers or something."

"Buck Rogers?" Helen echoed.

Billy suddenly looked very nervous. "I mean 'Star Trek.' Something like that. He's got a great imagination, has Jamey. Though he shouldn't oughta have pulled your leg, Ms. Emerson. I'll tell him so, when he gets back."

The more Billy babbled, the worse it got. Helen sat in the chair as numb fear washed over her. "When was Rafferty born, Billy?"

"November 4."

"What year?" she pushed it.

"Eighteen ninety...I mean, nineteen...er... uh... Hell, I don't know," Billy said frantically. "I was never any good at math."

"I'll make it easy on you. What year were you born?"

"Nineteen sixty-seven," he said quickly.

"You memorized that one."

"Ms. Emerson," he said earnestly, "don't ask questions when you don't want to know the answers. Or when you don't want to believe the answers. Just leave things as they are, okay, and everything will be fine. Rafferty will take care of business, and you'll be safe."

"What's he planning on doing?" The fear that was trickling down her spine was now increasing to a rush of panic.

"Look, just mellow out. Everything's copacetic." He didn't even seem to realize how out of place his words were. "He'll be back in no time."

"And if he's not?"

"Then we'll have to think of another way to get you out of here," Billy said.

The day's newspaper was lying folded on the table beside the visitor's chair. "Okay," she said. "I'll just sit here and read the paper, until you decide to tell me the truth."

"Billy!" Mary's voice was sharp with warning. The baby awoke with a shrill cry, just as Billy dove for the newspaper.

Helen was too fast for him. She flipped it open, staring at the headlines, the grainy photos, with no recognition whatsoever.

"Why don't you want me to read the paper?" she asked calmly, holding it tightly. "Am I supposed to be surprised by the state of the economy or political corruption?"

"It's just bad news, Ms. Emerson," Billy said. "Give it back to me and I'll toss it."

"I'd rather find out what it is you don't want me to see," she said, flipping open the first page.

It was there, right in front of her. A feature article about Chicago's most famous Valentine's Day, complete with police file photos. There was a grainy shot of a row of bodies, lined up on a cement floor. Beneath it were period photos of Al Capone and Bugs Moran. And a smaller photo of a man who could be none other than Willie Morris.

"Oh, God," Helen said in a quiet, horrified voice. She stared at the blurred photo of the dead bodies, and she could see one who looked eerily like the man standing across from her, misery on his young face.

She looked up at him. "It can't be true," she said flatly, still fighting it.

Billy moved to Mary's bedside, taking his wife's hand in his and squeezing tightly. "I don't know what I can tell you, Ms. Emerson."

"Tell me where Rafferty is."

"He had a few errands..."

"No," she said sharply. "In the picture. I don't see Rafferty's body."

Billy swallowed. "He...didn't die right away. He managed to crawl to the door of the garage. The police found him there."

"Oh, God," Helen whispered, shoving her fist into her mouth to stifle the urge to scream.

"Listen, no one knows why this happened to us," Billy said earnestly. "Least of all Rafferty. He was the best of us—he kept away from the dirty parts of the business, said no when the rest of us didn't dare. But we've all come through, all except for him. He must care about you, if he was able to tell you the truth."

"Where is he now?" She marveled at how calm she sounded. How rational.

"He's gone after Drago."

"No!" she cried, leaping from the chair and heading for the door.

Billy was ahead of her, stopping her, and he was stronger than he'd seemed. "I promised I'd keep you here until he got back, Ms. Emerson. I'd never break my promise to a man like Rafferty. He'll stop Drago. If he can't, no one can, and you're a dead woman. I don't think Rafferty could handle that."

"I can't let him . . ."

"No one lets Rafferty do anything. He decides," Billy overrode her, looking stubborn. "If he's not back by eleven o'clock, you're supposed to change into a nurse's uniform he stole for you. Then you hide out under the bed until your family can come get you."

Helen was five feet nine, and slender. Billy was an inch taller, scrappy, a street fighter. Helen was no match for him, but she didn't even hesitate.

She shoved her fist into his belly, hard, surprising him more than hurting him, and he doubled over just enough for her to take him off guard, hauling him out of the way and racing into the corridor. There was no sign of Rafferty's tall, wiry body, no sign of anyone familiar. The door opened behind her, but she took off, speeding down the hallway with a blind disregard for new mothers taking an early constitutional.

She could hear Billy thundering after her, but she ignored him, listening to her instincts, determined to find Rafferty before he could disappear, before he could make the ultimate sacrifice. The corridors were endless, crowded, anonymous, with no sign of him.

She had her choice—the elevators or the stairs. She headed for the stairs, for the door that was left ajar, taking them two at a time, her sneakered feet thudding on the metal treads, her breath rasping in her throat as she climbed upward, upward, uncertain of what she would find, terrified that she would only face death. Following her instincts and her heart in her need to reach Jamey Rafferty.

She reached the top floor, the landing dark and deserted, the light bulb burned out. She reached for the door, but it was locked, trapping her in the darkness. And behind her she could hear footsteps, slow, steady, deadly.

She yanked again at the door to the top floor, panicked, and this time it opened. She fell into the corridor, and hands caught her, hard, painful hands, wrapped around her wrists like manacles in the darkness.

"Damn it, Helen," Rafferty cursed, hauling her upright. "What are you doing here?"

The top floor of the hospital was deserted, the halls lined with storage, only a dim light illuminating the space. She stared up at him, at a man from another time and place, and her fear vanished. "I was looking for you."

He closed his eyes in brief exasperation, then shook her, hard. "I'm trying to save your life. I told Billy to keep you safe...."

"He did his best. I punched him in the stomach."

"Helen," he said, shaking his head in despair. "Mary's not going to thank you for that. You've got to get out of here. Go back to Mary's room and hide. I don't know when Drago's going to show up, I only know it's going to be tonight. This isn't a game we're playing, even if you don't want to believe me. I've known Drago for longer than you could believe possible, and he hates me almost as much as he hates you. He wants to kill you while I'm around, so that he can get the pleasure of watching my reaction."

She didn't move, taking what small comfort she could from his hard hands on her arms. "What makes him think you'll care that much?" she asked, aware of the absurdity of this conversation in a darkened, deserted hospital hallway, talking with a man returned from the dead, asking questions while a madman stalked her.

"He knows me." Rafferty's voice was bleak.

"And he knows what a knight in shining armor you are beneath your gangster pinstripes?" she said.

"No." He released her wrists, pushing his hands through her thick brown hair, running his thumbs across her soft lips. "He knows me better than that. He knows I've finally found my fatal weakness. If he kills you, then he destroys me, much more effectively than a hundred tommy gun bullets ripping into my flesh."

Helen shivered. "It's true, isn't it? You weren't making it up? I saw a picture..."

"Don't think about it, Helen," he said. "Don't think about any of this. It's just a bad dream, a nightmare, like your dreams about gunfire and dogs howling. It happened a long time ago—you don't have to worry about it, you don't have to think about it. All you have to think about is this." He put his mouth against her, gently, his tongue touching her lips, and she sank against him with a shaken sob, clutching him tightly, so tightly, as if she could fight the twisted whims of fate and fortune.

He kissed her cheekbones, her eyelids, her temples and her earlobes. He kissed her neck, her shoulders, he pulled her hips tight against his, so that she could feel how much he wanted her, and her own response heated and flowed, longing for him.

When he finally broke the kiss his expression was that still, scary one that no longer had the power to unnerve her. Except that she knew the determination that lay behind it.

"I want you to go now," he said, pulling her hands from around his neck, where she wanted to cling forever. "I want you to go back down those stairs and forget about me. There's no way we can change it, even if we wanted to."

"Even if we wanted to...?" she echoed, incensed.

"You deserve better than me, counselor," he said, and his mocking smile was back in full force. "You deserve someone noble and pure, someone who can give you the things you deserve...."

"You deserve a brain transplant," she snapped back. "How dare you tell me what I want, when what I want, what I need, what I deserve is you   "

"I didn't know they did brain transplants," he interrupted, the humor reaching his eyes as she fought for him.

"They don't. But I'm proposing you for the first candidate. I love you, Jamey. Haven't you listened to a word I've said? I love you, I love you, I love..."

His mouth silenced her, hard and hot and wet. He pushed her against the wall and kissed her as if his life depended on it, kissed her as if it were his last act on this earth. He kissed her with his heart and his soul, his tongue and his lips, his body and his mind, and she thought she might climax from the sheer power of it.

"Go away," he said, breaking away from her.

"I can't."

"Damn it, Helen . . ."

"Damn it, Rafferty," she mocked, no longer caring. "I can't go back down the stairs."

"Why not?"

"Because someone was following me. And I'm pretty sure it was Drago."

And then she was frightened. By the murderously bleak expression on his face. The resignation in his strong, lean body, and she had the sudden, hideous feeling that things were spinning out of her control, that death and despair were approaching from that deserted stairwell, and nothing Rafferty could do would stop it.

They heard the noise together, the scrape of footsteps, the turning of the doorknob. "Run," Rafferty ordered in a harsh whisper. "Run like hell." And he pulled her gun out of his coat pocket, holding it with both hands, training it toward the door.

Helen couldn't move, sickened, terrified. "Have you ever killed anyone before?" she asked.

"Yes."

"Rafferty . . ."

"Run, damn it."

Helen wheeled around, finally prepared to obey. Only to come face-to-face with Ricky Drago's mad eyes.

It all happened in slow motion, and yet at lightning speed. Helen screamed, in warning, in terror, just as Billy's voice could be heard on the other side of the locked door, pounding, calling to Rafferty. Rafferty whirled around, aiming the gun, but Drago had already caught Helen, hauling her up against him, using her as a shield.

"Too bad, Rafferty," Drago said with a wheezy little chuckle. "I didn't want to play it this way. But you've been too good. You always were. Maybe this time you'll finally get the peace you deserve." And raising the gun he held in his right hand, he aimed it point-blank at Rafferty's face.

And fired it.

Chapter Thirteen

Rafferty was dead. There was no other possibility, not with a gun fired at point-blank range. Helen's mind accepted that unalterable truth, even as her heart fought it. She screamed, kicking and clawing at Drago, desperate to get to Rafferty's fallen body, but even in her wild state Drago was too strong for her. She half expected him to use that gun on her, the gun that smelled of cordite and death, and she didn't care. She wanted to be with Rafferty, and if he was dead then her own life had little meaning.

She yanked herself away, stumbling to her knees beside his body, flinging herself on top of him as he lay facedown on the linoleum floor. Behind the door she could still hear Billy, shouting, and with her last ounce of energy she screamed out a warning. She didn't even see the gun coming, feel it slam against the side of her head. All she knew was blackness.

She floated for a while, in a sea of loss and confusion. She knew someone was carrying her, someone she hated. She could feel the hardness of a shoulder digging into her stomach, hear the muffled grunts as she was hoisted through space. She wondered whether she were dead, whether she was going to find Rafferty in this dreamlike limbo. Whether they'd return together, every Valentine's Day, to live out the last two days of their lives.

In her dreamlike state she no longer had any doubt that Rafferty had told her the truth. It all made its own weird kind of sense. But there were still a thousand questions unanswered. Had she joined Rafferty in death? Or was Rafferty somewhere else, his endless cycle of Valentine Days over with at last?

Everything hurt. Her head, her heart, her mind and soul. She couldn't, wouldn't think about it. The blackness beckoned, a safe, nurturing blackness, far away from the labored giggles of the madman who carried her. And she welcomed the blackness, searching for Rafferty within its velvet confines.

BILLY SLAMMED THROUGH the safety door, coming in low to avoid gunfire. In the shadowy stillness of the unused hospital corridor he thought at first that it was deserted. Until he saw Rafferty lying facedown, unmoving.

"God, no!" Billy moaned, running to his side, tugging at him. The sound of gunfire had filled him with dread—Drago wasn't the kind of man who missed often, and according to Rafferty, he'd missed twice in the past two days. He wouldn't be making another mistake.

He turned Rafferty over, staring down into his un-marked face. There was no sign of a bullet wound, no sign of any trauma. He lay very still, and Billy put his head against Rafferty's chest, listening for a heart-beat.

It was there, quite faint, but growing steadily stronger. There was no blood, no sign of a scuffle. Just Rafferty lying there, as still and silent as the grave.

"What . . . what the hell are you doing?" his voice wheezed, and Billy sat back, relief washing over him.

"You're not dead," he said foolishly, backhanding an unmanly tear from his eye.

"That's a matter of opinion," Rafferty said, his wry voice sounding hoarser than usual. "What hap-pened?"

"Beats me. I was trying to catch up with Ms. Emerson. The door was locked, and I heard you shouting at her, and then a gunshot." He glanced around him. "Where is she? Did Drago shoot her? What happened . . . ?"

Rafferty closed his eyes and began to curse, some-thing far more intense than the mild "damn its" he'd favored Helen with. "Drago's got her," he snapped, surging to his feet, swaying slightly for a moment. "And I'm the one he shot."

"Jeez, Rafferty!" Billy gasped, putting a support-ing hand under his arm. "Where . . . how . . . are you okay?"

Rafferty shook himself, almost in disbelief. "I'm okay," he said. "After all this time I should be get-ting used to crazy things, but I'm not. Drago shot me right between the eyes,'' he said, staring at Billy with his unmarked face. "I heard the noise, felt the heat and pressure of the bullet. And all I've got right now is one hell of a headache.''

"Does that mean he can't hurt Ms. Emerson?''

"Who the hell knows what any of this means?'' Rafferty countered wearily. "I don't trust fate, or providence, or Drago's aim. We've got to get her, and we've got to stop Drago, or maybe the next person he shoots won't have my amazing recuperative powers.'' The heavy mockery in his voice couldn't quite disguise the fear.

"Where do you think he took her? I only heard one gunshot, so she must still be okay. Unless he used a knife..." Billy let the words trail off as he recognized Rafferty's expression. He'd known Rafferty for more than half a century, and he had thought that eerie stillness of his had lost the power to frighten him. He was mistaken.

"She's all right,'' Rafferty said in a quiet, deadly voice. "She's hurt, she's frightened, but she's still all right.''

"You know that?'' Billy asked, all admiration. There seemed to be no end to Rafferty's powers.

"No,'' he said, disillusioning him. "But the alternatives are unacceptable. Helen's okay. She has to be.''

And Billy wasn't about to put up an argument. "Where do you think he's taking her? Maybe we can head him off.''

Rafferty slammed his fist against the wall with impotent rage, and Billy noticed for the first time that he was still holding the gun. "Why the hell can't I think straight?" Rafferty said. "I don't think he'd go back to Clark Street—he tried that once, and it failed. There's just an old folks home there now, anyway." He tucked the gun into his waistband. "We'll start at his place and go from there. Since he took her with him instead of killing her here, he must have something in mind. Are you coming with me?"

"Is the pope Catholic?"

"What the hell does the pope have to do with anything?" Rafferty snapped, heading down the hallway at an uneven run.

"Sorry," Billy muttered, abashed, as he followed him. "It's just a saying. Does that gun work?"

"Not for me. I tried when I saw Drago grab Helen. It wouldn't even cock. You want to use it?"

"Not if I can help it. My parole is pretty shaky at this point—if I'm caught with a loaded weapon I'm looking at some hard time."

Rafferty stopped and stared at him. "You'd let Helen die?"

"No. But I'm looking for alternatives that'll keep us all alive. You included."

Rafferty's smile was bleak and humorless. "It's too late for me. We figured that out a long time ago. The rules don't apply to me. All I need to do is get Drago. If I can accomplish that much, I don't give a damn whether I come back anymore."

"But she'll wait for you. She might not believe . . ."

"I don't want her waiting. I'm no good for her, Billy. She deserves the best, not some remnant of another time and place, a time and place better left forgotten. Even if I had the choice, I'd choose to leave."

"You're in love with her," Billy said, his voice soft with astonishment.

"It's that obvious?"

"To someone who knows you," Billy said. "Mary said something about it, but I thought she was just being crazy after the baby's birth. Did you tell her?"

"Tell who? Ms. Emerson? Of course not. She doesn't need that kind of complication in her life. Once I'm gone she'll convince herself that it was all a dream. At least some of the more unlikely aspects of our time together. By next fall she'll be ready to move on."

"You're awful dumb for such a smart man, Rafferty," Billy said.

"I've got to find her, Billy. I've got to save her life," Rafferty said, his voice bleak and desperate. "Help me figure out where to start."

Billy shook his head. "I haven't got the faintest idea. You're the one who seems so tuned in on her. Listen to your heart."

"I don't have one," Rafferty said.

"Don't give me that. Use your instincts, man. Sixty-five years ago you had the most powerful instincts in Chicago. Bugs Moran wouldn't spit if you didn't tell him it would be okay, Capone was shivering in his fancy boots at the thought of you. You've got talent, you've got a gift. Use it," Billy said.

Rafferty leaned against the wall by the freight elevator, closing his eyes. "It never mattered so much before, Billy," he said in a hard, quiet voice. "If I make a mistake this time, it's for keeps."

"You won't make a mistake, Rafferty. You're here to save her life. You're here to make her life. Don't blow it."

Rafferty's eyes flew open, and for the first and only time in his life Billy saw fear there. Uncertainty, strength and love as well. "I know where he took her," he said, and the moment of fear was gone.

"Then what the hell are we waiting for?" Billy said. "Let's do it."

"Do it?" Rafferty echoed, punching the elevator button. "What's that supposed to mean?"

Billy found he could smile. The night was far from over, and before it ended there would be blood and death. But he was a survivor, and so was Rafferty. They'd been through too much, too many lifetimes, to let it go now. When the smoke cleared, Drago would be dead, this time for good. And with any luck at all, Rafferty would still be here.

"You'll learn, Rafferty," he promised, thinking of all the tomorrows. "You'll learn."

HELEN WAS COLD, miserably, achingly cold. She didn't want to open her eyes, wasn't even sure they would open. Her eyelids felt frozen, her toes were blocks of ice and her fingers were numb. She huddled against the brick, wondering if the ice on her face was frozen tears. And then she realized it was wet snow, plastering her skin.

She didn't move. She'd left her down coat in Mary Moretti's hospital room, but she didn't particularly care. Freezing to death was supposed to be a comparatively pleasant way to go. Everything went numb, and you felt sort of drunk, and then you just drifted off to sleep. She wasn't sure if that was taking into account the bitter wind that was ripping through her thick cotton sweater, slicing through her baggy jeans. She could have done without that. She would have preferred being blanketed in a layer of thick new snow, wrapped in a cocoon of whiteness, where she could lie like some medieval maiden, waiting for her knight errant to return from the crusades.

"You awake, lady?" Ricky Drago's high, unpleasantly cheerful voice broke through her fantasy, and she decided to ignore him, seeing if she could summon back the hazy vision of Rafferty.

"Hey, lady." His hand caught her chin, squeezing it painfully, and her eyes flew open, blinking away the snowflakes that had lodged in her lashes. "That's better," Drago said. "I don't want you out of it. Not yet, at least. I've got plans for you. Big plans."

She just stared at him. There was nothing worse he could do to her, she reminded herself. He'd murdered Rafferty—life could offer no crueler surprises.

Drago didn't like her silence. His fingers tightened cruelly, and she let out a small, involuntary whimper. "That's better," he crooned. "You don't like pain, Ms. Emerson? Few people do. I like it. I like to watch it. I like to make people hurt. I always have. It's something wrong with me, my mother told me that. She used to try to beat it out of me, but it never worked. You can't beat meanness out of a kid, Ms. Emerson. You just beat it in deeper."

She didn't want to say anything, but she knew he expected it, demanded it, and she was finding the pain almost unbearable. "You're right," she managed to croak out.

He laughed then, a high, eerie sound in the night air. "I'm right?" he echoed. "What do you know about meanness, Ms. Emerson? What do you know about what life does to you? You just sit behind your desk and ask your questions and you never listen to the answers. You make someone so damned mad that he... It was your fault." He switched track abruptly. "All your fault, not mine."

Despite the pain in her head, the iciness of her heart, she had no trouble following his rambling train of thought. "I'm sorry about your wife," she said, not knowing what name to call him.

He slapped her. Her head whipped sideways, her cheek grazed the brick wall that she was huddled against and her eyes stung with tears of pain. "You're sorry," he said in an awful, hissing voice. "You don't even know what sorry will begin to feel like. You're going to discover new levels of regret that no one ever thought possible. I'm good at what I do, Ms. Emerson. I was one of the best, in a time when there were a lot of experts in my field. And I haven't lost my touch. But you don't know what I'm talking about, do you?

Rafferty never tells anyone. You want to know why? He can't. It's that simple. None of us could. It would have given us an unfair advantage. Only after I found Lizzie, after she showed me how things could be...how..." His voice trailed off again, and the sorrow and despair on his mad face were truly devastating.

"What are you going to do to me?" she asked, unable to keep her voice from shaking. It was the cold she told herself, knowing it was the fear.

The sorrow vanished from Ricky Drago's face, replaced by a look of gleeful cunning. "I would have thought that was obvious. I'm going to kill you. You're responsible for my wife's death, and you have to pay. It's been made very clear to me. You pay for the sins you commit. I've had to pay, and now it's your turn, Ms. Emerson."

She looked past him. Snow was coming down heavily, layering his thinning black hair, coating his leather jacket. Ricky Drago was no formal throwback to the twenties, Chicago style. He was every inch a modern hood, with murder on his mind. Rafferty's murder, already accomplished. And hers.

"What's keeping you then?" she demanded, no longer caring. It had to be well below freezing, and with the windchill factor she'd probably freeze to death before long. Not that such an end might not be preferable, but she was getting heartily sick of Drago. "You've killed Rafferty, why don't you finish me off?"

"You'd like that, wouldn't you? But I've bungled the job three times already. I'm not about to make another mistake. I'm going to savor the moment, do it right. And I want to give him enough time to get here if he's smart enough to figure it out."

"Who?" she asked numbly.

"Rafferty."

"He's dead," she said, fighting against the sudden surge of hope. "I saw you shoot him in the face. No one could survive..."

"Probably not," he agreed. "But Rafferty is full of surprises. I think we'll give him a little time. See if he still has the ability to rise from the dead." And he laughed, a high-pitched, eerie giggle that made Helen's skin crawl.

He'd warned her about regret, about sadistic pain. He'd just delivered her the cruelest blow imaginable—impossible hope. "Where are we?" she demanded, staring around her. Even coated in icy white, the bleak landscape looked familiar. A snow-capped desert, with strange shapes looming beyond them, she'd been there before, in another time, another place. Just like Rafferty.

"Don't you recognize it?" Drago said, sitting back on his heels in the gathering snow. "It's your rooftop, Ms. Emerson. You used to come out here in the summer and lie on a towel and unfasten the top of your bathing suit. I watched you. I was waiting, waiting for the right time. Did you know I was watching you? Waiting for you to sit up and show me your breasts? Did you show Rafferty your breasts, Ms. Emerson?''

Helen fought down the sudden panicked nausea at the thought of him, watching. ''Why didn't you kill me then?''

Drago shrugged. ''Like I said, the time wasn't right. I was planning on waiting for Valentine's Day. For old time's sake. I haven't whacked anyone since I came back, and I thought you'd be the perfect one to start with.''

''But you started with Rafferty.''

Drago's face darkened. ''Yeah,'' he said. ''I didn't want to do that. I mean, things were working out pretty good. I never thought that dope Billy would really get you two together, but he did. He never knew that's what I had in mind in the first place. I really wanted to do you both at the same time. But then, life is full of little disappointments. I may still get the chance.''

''Why did you want to kill Rafferty? What did he ever do to you . . . ?''

Drago's smile was very sweet. ''It's like what they say about climbing Mount Everest. You do it because it's there. Rafferty was always a boil on my butt. All he ever had to do was look at someone and he'd scare the hell out of them. I had to use force.''

''Didn't you want to?''

''Yeah,'' he said, after he thought about it. ''Good point. But then, nobody ever said you were stupid, Ms. Emerson.''

She didn't know how much longer this could go on, carrying on a crazy conversation with a madman. Where was the drifting, cloudlike comfort of freezing to death? She was so cold she ached, a hard, solid pain that wouldn't stop, that matched the throbbing in her head, the stinging in her cheek, the icy numbness in her hands and feet, the devastating hole in her heart. She wanted it over, she wanted safety and comfort and Rafferty's arms around her. If death was the only way she could have it, then death it was.

"Are you sure you want to wait, Ricky?" she asked in a taunting voice. "What if Rafferty does manage to survive? What if he shows up here, maybe with Billy? Do you want to take that chance? It must be strange to fail, after being such an expert in your field. Don't you want to prove to yourself you can still do it?"

Drago was looking at her with astonishment wiping out some of his eerie glee. "What did you call me?" he asked hoarsely.

"Ricky. Ricky Drago's your real name, isn't it? Not Willie Morris."

He suddenly looked very pale. "How did you know that? It's not in my police records. It's not anywhere." He grabbed her shoulders, squeezing hard, and shook her. "How the hell did you know my real name?" he shouted in her face.

"Rafferty told me."

He flung her back against the brick wall. "He couldn't have. That's not the way it's supposed to work."

"You want to keep it a secret, Drago? Then you should have done something about the newspapers. There's a couple of pictures of you in today's *Chronicle*—Billy showed them to me. One of you from 1928, all spiffy and elegant. And another one a year later, lying dead on a garage floor."

"Bitch," Drago said viciously.

"Why do you waste your time with me, Ricky? Why do you waste your time with someone like Rafferty? Wouldn't you be better off tracking down the men who shot you sixty some years ago?"

"You stupid fool. They're all dead. They've been dead almost as long as we have, and they haven't come back. Don't ask me why. I hunted for them, every year, even caught up with a couple of them, and it was no good. I couldn't kill them. Just as I know Rafferty can't kill me. He may want to stop me, but there's not a damned thing he can do. All he can do is watch as I kill you."

"But he's already dead."

"Maybe. Maybe not. I'm keeping an open mind. We'll wait."

"I'm cold," she said, her voice trembling with shivers.

"Too bad you don't have Crystal's old coat. Maybe I should consider going downstairs and getting it. There'd be a certain justice in that. Crystal was always sweet to me. Treated me real nice. Except that she treated Rafferty even nicer."

"Is that why you want to kill him?"

"Hell, no," Drago said, some of his former good cheer returning. "It just seems like the thing to do. Then maybe when I finish with the two of you I'll go after Moretti. Can't trust the little snitch."

"He didn't tell me about you," Helen said, as panic whipped through her. "He refused to cooperate when he was arrested this last time."

"Then why did you let him walk?"

"Rafferty..."

"It doesn't matter. I think I'm developing a taste for this. I didn't get to enjoy doing Rafferty, but I'm going to enjoy you. And then..."

"Get away from her." It wasn't Rafferty's voice in the snow-whipped stillness. It was Billy's, sounding hoarse, determined, and deadly. Helen squinted into the darkness, but she couldn't see a thing.

Drago didn't turn around. He stayed where he was, squatting on his haunches in front of her, and the muzzle of the gun was pressed underneath her chin. "You can't stop me, Billy," he scoffed. "I remember the time you puked, when we had that shoot-out over on Sycamore. You're not the killing type, and you know it as well as I do. Maybe to save your wife and child, but what the hell do you care about a state's attorney? She tried to keep you away from Mary. If she lives, she's your natural enemy."

"Get away from her, Ricky." Helen's weary eyes followed the sound of Billy's voice. He was off to the right, silhouetted against the blue-black sky, the snow swirling around him.

Drago knew where he was as well. "Make me, Billy," he said, turning his head in Billy's direction.

And then Helen saw him. Coming up on the other side, silent, as still as always, stalking his enemy, and she couldn't control her little start of joy and disbelief.

It was enough to alert Drago. He yanked the gun from underneath her chin, fired it at Billy, then whirled around to face the approaching figure, the burning metal against Helen's temple, scorching her. "I'm going to kill her, Rafferty," he wheezed. "You've made my dreams come true. You can't stop me, and even if I can't kill you, in another few hours you'll be gone. But don't worry about it. I'll be waiting for you next Valentine's Day. I'll have something really festive planned."

Rafferty stepped into the light, and Helen sucked in her breath as she saw his face. There was no mark on it from the gun that had been fired point-blank at him. No mark, but a deadly purpose.

"You want to die, Drago?" he asked, his voice soft and menacing. "Stupid question—of course you want to die. You want to be with Lizzie again. Let Helen go. There are police crawling all over this building. Didn't you know Ms. Emerson comes from a family of cops? All it took was one phone call and half the force is on its way."

"Do you think I care? Cops couldn't touch me back then—they won't get me now." He stroked the gun against Helen's cheek, and it was all she could do not to scream.

"You're not invulnerable, Ricky. I'm one up on you that way. We're a little more evenly matched this time. Stop hiding behind your hostage. Are you afraid of me? Afraid that this time I might be able to do it?"

"You can't take me," Drago said in a high-pitched shriek, pushing Helen away and rising to his feet. "I'm not afraid of anything, and I'm not afraid of an East Coast jerk like you, with your fancy clothes and your fancy ways. You think you had Moran fooled, but he laughed at you behind your back. We all did. We knew you didn't have the guts when things got rough. You didn't refuse out of scruples, you refused to go along with the rough stuff because you were scared. You couldn't shoot a living soul...."

Rafferty raised the gun in his hand, pointing it at Drago. "But then, who knows if you qualify as a living soul, Ricky," he said in a shivery, gentle tone of voice, aiming the gun. "Let's see." And the sound of the gun being cocked in the stillness was as audible as an actual firing.

Drago's face turned sickly white. "You can't," he gasped, taking a step backward, forgetting about Helen. "After all these years..."

"After all these years," Rafferty said, advancing on him, a slow, steady pace that drove all thought of his hostage out of Drago's deranged mind, "I finally can."

And then Drago smiled, a ghastly travesty of humor. "No, you can't," he said. "Not if I'm not threatening your little lady friend. You can't shoot me in cold blood, even if you know I deserve it." He took another, deliberate step away from Helen, holding his arms up, the gun still in one hand. "Go ahead, Rafferty. Let's see if you can play the cosmic avenger."

He couldn't do it. Helen knew it, Drago knew it. Rafferty couldn't shoot him down in cold blood, and that fact was his salvation. And their possible doom. The gun wavered in Rafferty's strong hand, then lowered as he released the firing mechanism. "Get the hell out of here, Drago," he said wearily.

"No way." He whirled around, the gun raised and aimed straight at Helen's head, when a volley of shots filled the air. She knew that sound, the noise of a thousand drumbeats, the roar of thunder, as Drago's body was riddled with bullets. And then all was an eerie silence.

Helen reached Drago's body at the same moment Rafferty did, and Rafferty took his hand, holding it hard. "Damn," Drago wheezed. "Who would have thunk it? A copper finally got me in the end. See you, Raff..." His voice trailed off into silence. An eternal one. And Helen knew with absolute certainty that there would be no more valentines for Ricky Drago.

There were police all around her, pulling her away from the body, pulling her away from Rafferty. She knew half of them, but at least none of her family was present.

"I'm okay," she said as someone tried to check her. "What about Billy?"

"Just a flesh wound." It was Rafferty's voice behind her, a voice she never thought to hear again. "They'll take him to the same hospital as Mary."

She turned to look at him across the crowded rooftop. Ignoring a dozen curious cops, she ran into his arms, holding tight, hiding her face against his chest.

And somewhere in the wintry silence, a dog began to howl.

Chapter Fourteen

The apartment was still and silent when Rafferty finally shut the door behind them. He didn't bother to switch on the light, and the darkness was a blessed relief to Helen's ragged nerves. She slumped against him, exhausted, too weary even to cry, and his arms were tight, strong, comforting. The beat of his heart was slow and steady beneath her ear, the heat of him was palpable through his formal clothes. He was real, he was there. But for how long?

She tried to remember Billy's words to her as they'd bundled him onto a stretcher. He'd been pale, in shock, but he'd managed a weak smile. "Don't think about it," he whispered. "That's what Mary wanted me to tell you. Just take each moment as it comes, and don't think about the past. It's too crazy. Take what you can and hold on to it."

Helen was trying to do just that. The last day and a half seemed nothing short of insane—a dreamlike excursion from reality that both exhausted and overwhelmed her. She never wanted it to end. And if she could believe Rafferty, it was about to end, all too soon.

"Billy will be all right," Rafferty murmured into her hair, his hands strong and comforting on her narrow back. She was huddled into his overcoat, and his own clothes were wet from melted snow. She sighed, pressing against him, wanting to absorb herself into his very bones.

Rafferty's powers never ceased to amaze Helen. His ability to return from the dead, to take a bullet in the face with no aftereffect were impressive enough. His ability to withstand the assembled, familial power of the Chicago police department was nothing short of miraculous.

He might not have been quite so successful at expediting the removal of Drago's body and sending the dozen police on their way with promises of full cooperation if members of her immediate family had been present. As it was, there were two honorary uncles, three ex-partners and a couple of patrolmen she'd worked with in the past, all with a personal interest in Helen's well-being and an instinctive distrust for the still, silent stranger who was overruling them.

Rafferty won. Once Billy was stabilized, his color pale but his pulse steady, once the initial questions were answered, Rafferty simply got rid of them. And no one, up to and including honorary uncle Tommy Lapatrie who'd bounced baby Helen on his knee after her christening could stand up to him.

"I keep thinking about Drago," she whispered in the darkness, pressing her face against his damp white

shirt, his warm chest. "To see him cut down like
that. . . . " She shuddered, and Rafferty's hold tightened. "Did they have to use machine guns?" she
whispered.

"They didn't."

She raised her head, as a fresh chill ran through her
body. "What do you mean? I heard them, I saw
them . . ."

"A police sharpshooter killed him. Three bullets,
just to make certain."

"But I heard . . . And the dog . . ." she said.

"Don't think about it, Helen. It was another time,
another place. Drago is where he belongs now, and if
you ask me, he's happy to be there. Losing his wife put
him back over the edge. Now he can rest."

She looked up at him. "Is that supposed to be
comforting?" she asked. "Is that what you're expecting? A nice, eternal rest? If I can believe what you've
been telling me . . ."

"Don't believe a word I've said." He cupped her
face with his strong hands, running his sensitive
thumbs across her trembling mouth. "It's all a pack
of lies. Just believe in the moment. That's all anyone
ever has."

"That's what Billy told me," Helen whispered,
looking into his bleak, sorrow-filled eyes.

"Billy would know."

"I just have one question."

"Don't ask it," Rafferty said, his voice desperate.
"It will only make things worse. Either I'll lie to you,

and you'll hate me, or I'll tell you the truth, and you'll wind up hating me anyway."

"I'm not going to ask if you love me, Jamey," she managed a pragmatic tone of voice, and his mouth began to curve in a reluctant smile. "I know the answer, even if you don't. I just want to know if you'd stay. If it were up to you."

"I don't think I should answer that, either."

She reached up and took his face in her hands, his dear, lost face. "I'm not giving you a choice, mister," she said firmly. "Would you stay?"

For a moment he didn't say a word. And then he closed his eyes, and she could see his soul flash across the dark planes of his face. "Wild horses couldn't drag me away."

From somewhere in the distance they could hear the sound of Crystal's grandfather clock, beginning the slow, sad chime of midnight. "Are you about to turn into a pumpkin?" she whispered, her fingers tightening.

He shook his head. "By tomorrow morning," he said, his voice rough.

"Then we have time? A few more hours?"

"A few more hours," Rafferty said.

"It will have to be enough." She reached up and kissed him, her mouth open against his, tasting his darkness and sorrow, tasting the decades.

The apartment was warm and dark and safe. Outside the storm raged, inside all was heat and flesh and love. She wasn't quite sure how they made it into the bedroom. She was trembling as she closed the door behind them and began to strip the clothes off him, pushing his jacket and shirt onto the floor, reaching for his belt buckle. She half expected him to protest, to take control, but he seemed to know she had to be the one to take the lead, to touch, to kiss, to run her mouth down his chest to the waistband of his trousers, to unfasten the unexpected row of buttons, to touch him, hold him, reveling in the warmth and strength of him, in his muffled groan of pleasure. He was like silk and steel in her hand, pulsing with desire, and she wanted more. In the few short hours remaining she wanted everything, a lifetime to last her through the long empty nights that stretched ahead of her, without him. She'd waited twenty-nine years for him. She wasn't about to settle for anything less.

"Take off your clothes," he said, and his voice was rough in the moonlit darkness, rough and caressing.

She obeyed, pulling the baggy sweater over her head, skimming her jeans down over her hips and kicking them away. She reached up to undo the front clasp of her thin scrap of a bra, but his large hand covered hers, stopping her, and he drew her closer, putting his hot, wet mouth over her breast, suckling it through the wisp of lace that covered her.

His hands slid down her sides, along her hips beneath the silk panties, cupping her, pulling her against him. Her knees felt weak, trembly, her heart was racing, her pulses were full and flowing. She was overwhelmed with longings so fierce, so intense that she was afraid she might fly apart. She needed him, all of him, in every way possible. She wanted him hard and fast, she wanted him slow and lingering. She wanted forever. And she only had one more night.

He kicked out of the rest of his clothes and pulled her over to the bed. She lay down with him, leaning over him as he lay back against the pillows, and her hair was a curtain around them, shutting out the cold February night. She kissed his lips, running her tongue along the firm edges of his mouth as he tried to kiss her back. She moved her mouth down the tautly muscled planes of his chest, touching, tasting, savoring him, storing a thousand sensations inside her. She kissed his stomach, his navel, his hips. And then she put her mouth on him, feeling him jerk with surprise, his hands threading her hair, holding her there, gently, as she loved him, she loved him, and she never wanted it to end.

She was trembling, covered with sweat, when he pulled her away, and she fought for a moment. "Wait," she said. "I want to..."

"I want to come inside you," Rafferty said. "Not just your mouth. I need all of you. Now." He pulled her up and over him, so that she lay full-length on top of him, her hands clutching his shoulders.

He reached up and unfastened the bra she was still wearing. He pulled off her silk panties, roughly, and threw them off the bed. "I don't want to hurt you again," he said. "But I can't help it. It's too soon..."

"Show me," she said, overriding his concern. "We only have a few more hours. Show me what to do."

He groaned, and his last attempt at restraint vanished as he reached between her legs to the heated, aching center of her. She arched against his hand, whimpering softly with pleasure, and in the darkness he smiled, murmuring to her, telling her how sweet and responsive she was, how soft and sleek and damp and hot she was, and how much he needed, wanted her.

"Slowly, love," he whispered as he positioned her above him, throbbing and ready. "Very slowly. Make it last. God, Helen..." the words were a jumble of pleasure as she followed his lead, sinking slowly, filling herself with his strength.

There was no pain this time. Just a tightness, a stretching, followed by the most glorious burgeoning inside her as she flowed around him, her heart bursting, her soul in flight as he held her hips in his big hands and showed her a slow, steady rhythm that was likely to drive her mad. His control was greater than hers. When she was ready to shake apart, reaching for something beyond her grasp, he simply rolled her over on the bed, covering her, surging against her with a slow, steady pace that made her want to scream, to pound at his shoulders and weep.

And suddenly his control was gone as well, and he thrust into her, again and again, in a frenzy of need that brought forth her own wild response, and when he went rigid in her arms, his body arched against hers, his voice lost in a strangled cry, she was with him, shattering around him, tossed into the maelstrom of a love that knew no boundaries of time and space, life and death.

His hands were still tight on her, and she hoped he'd leave a mark, a bruise, anything to hold on to after he left. Something to remind herself that he'd really been here. His face was buried in her hair, his heart still racing against hers, and she wanted to cling so fiercely that all the forces of heaven and hell couldn't touch him. And death shall have no dominion—where did that line come from, Shakespeare or the Bible? She only wished it were true.

Eventually their breathing slowed. "I'm crushing you," he muttered into her hair, making no move to get off her.

"I'm glad. Don't leave." Her body made an involuntary jerk at her choice of words. "I mean, don't..."

"I know what you mean." He lifted his head, looking down at her, and for the first time his face was oddly peaceful. No dark mockery, no secrets lurking behind his eyes. "I didn't want to do this to you."

She found she could smile, still wrapped tightly in his embrace. "Really? You could have fooled me."

He kissed her, lightly touching her tender lips. "I didn't want to make love to you, and then leave you," he said patiently. "You deserve so much more...."

"True," she said, indulging in her own lighthearted mockery, "but I don't happen to want anyone but you. Will you come back to me? Next year?" She didn't bother to try to disguise the anxiety and need in her voice. He would have heard it anyway.

"I can't ask you to wait three hundred and sixty-five days..."

"Three hundred and sixty-three," she corrected. "And I've already waited twenty-nine years for you. What's another three hundred days, more or less?"

"Helen, I..."

This time she stopped him, putting her fingers against his mouth. "You didn't want to say that, remember?" she whispered. "Tell me when you come back. I'll be waiting for you."

"I don't want you to..."

"I'll be waiting," she said, implacably.

He closed his eyes, fighting it for one more moment. And then he opened them, and there was love and acceptance in the sunlit depths. "I'll be back."

"I know you will," she said, her voice sounding strange and deep to her own ears. "And this lifetime will be for us." She let her eyes drift closed, unable to keep them open a moment longer.

She didn't want to sleep. She didn't want to lose one second, one moment, one breath, one heartbeat. But her body had its own needs, its own wisdom. She'd just survived the most tumultuous forty-eight hours of her life, and she needed rest, renewal, no matter how much she fought against it. She closed her eyes, drinking in the weight of him against her, the scent of his skin, the sound of his breathing. And then she slept.

RAFFERTY WAITED until she was sound asleep, waited until he could wait no longer, and then he pulled out of her arms, gently, lying beside her, watching her in the moonlit darkness as she slept.

The snow had stopped long ago—even before they'd come down from the roof. The time up there seemed strange and distant. He'd never seen so many cops in one place at one time. It was enough to make him nervous.

But he hadn't been. He'd been too concerned with Helen, her face pale and crumpled, her muscles weak, her eyes wide and loving. Too concerned with his unbreakable date with destiny, and the need to cram every minute of living, of loving, in before he had to go.

He lay in bed with her now, touching her gently, pushing the hair away from her face. He could see a trace of dried tears on her cheeks, and he wanted to taste them. He was so hungry for her, so starved for her, that he could never get enough.

He couldn't rid himself of his sense of rightness, of belonging. He knew he should regret touching her, taking her, loving her. Knew he should regret the fact that she'd be waiting for him.

But he couldn't. Logic and should-have-beens had no place in his life. He only knew what was right. And Helen was right, for now and for always. Even if it was only forty-eight hours at a time.

He found himself thinking about Elena. With her pitch-black hair, bright blue eyes, her small, plump body and her old-world ways, she was as far removed from a modern woman like Helen Emerson as she could be.

Where had those words come from? The words of a woman long dead, a woman who'd never been his, except in his heart. Spoken in Elena's husky voice. The words of the woman he finally loved.

It made no sense, and he was far too weary to try to understand it. He'd fought for years, hoping to make sense of it, and no sense had emerged. He'd learned just to accept each day as it came.

He leaned over and feathered a kiss against Helen's bee-stung lips. He'd kissed her too hard, too often, and he wanted to kiss her again. But most of all he wanted to simply lie there and watch her, so that the last thing he saw was her peaceful, beautiful, sleeping face. To carry with him into his own tiny share of eternity.

He could feel it coming. It always started with sleep, with a bone-numbing exhaustion sweeping over him, one he was powerless to fight. It was sliding over him like a warm, soft blanket, comforting, enveloping, and even though he wanted to bat it away, to cling more tightly to Helen, he knew it would only make it worse. The best thing he could do for her was let it take him. Let her wake in the morning to an empty bed. And if he was really noble he'd hope that when he came back next year she'd have gone on with her life.

But he wasn't noble. And he knew she'd be waiting. And he closed his eyes, and let the darkness come.

THE LIGHT WAS BRILLIANT, bright white and blinding. Rafferty opened his eyes, blinking against the glare, covering his eyes with his arm. Beside him he felt someone move, heard a muffled curse.

He yanked his arm away, sitting up with a jerk. He was in the middle of Helen Emerson's bed, the white sheet pulled up over him, Helen curled up beside him, holding a pillow over her head as she tried to shut out the bright midwinter sun. The clock radio beside the bed said 9:05, and the voice of an announcer was a muffled rush of words.

He reached over and after several false starts managed to turn up the sound. "And it's another cold winter day in the Windy City," a man's voice said. "Sunday, February 15, and if you missed Valentine's Day this year, there's always another chance next year. This is Simon Zebriskie on WAKS, with you until eleven o'clock, and if you forgot to tell her you loved her, now's the time to do so. Maybe this will help."

Rafferty knew the song. It was an old one, though not as old as he was. "When a Man Loves a Woman."

He turned back to look at Helen. She'd emerged from the pillow, staring at him in joyous disbelief.

"You're still here," she said, her voice rusty.

He didn't bother to agree. "I love you," he said.

She smiled then, her smile as blazingly bright as the midwinter sun. "I know you do," she said, sitting up and holding the sheet around her in a belated show of modesty, and it took him a moment to realize that he was going to have time to teach her not to blush. To show her so many things that she'd become positively brazen. With him alone. "But I don't think I believe anything else you told me." Her voice was just the slightest bit uncertain.

"It's better that way," he said. "We get to start anew. We'll get married . . ."

"We'll have babies . . ."

"I'll find a job . . ."

"Mel Amberson already offered you one. . . ."

"I love you."

She leaned over and kissed him, dropping the sheet to her waist. "I love you, too," she murmured. "And you're going to love my family."

Rafferty remembered the small battalion of cops surrounding Helen, and stifled a groan. "Anything's possible," he muttered.

"Yes," she said happily, "it is." And the bright Chicago sunlight shone down on them through the window as they welcomed all their new tomorrows.

Epilogue

It was one more Valentine's Day, one year later. Like most Valentine's Days in Chicago, the day was cold and blustery, a light snow falling. For the first time in sixty-five years there were no more unexpected returns to Clark Street. Everyone, including Ricky Drago's tortured soul, had found its own kind of peace.

There'd been too many questions and not enough answers. Such as the mystery of a stolen car found dented and hot-wired outside the former site of the infamous St. Valentine's Day Massacre, with no fingerprints inside but those of a crook who'd been dead for almost seven decades.

Or the question of Rafferty's birth certificate, or any means of any formal identification when Helen and Jamey applied for a marriage license at the end of February. Fortunately a circuit court judge named Clarissa was willing to expedite matters and do them a favor, even if she had to fudge a bit, and the wedding went as planned, with Billy and Mary and Jamey Moretti in attendance, looking uneasily at the assembled, blue-coated Emersons across the aisle.

Rafferty discovered an almost indecent flair for the stock market under Mel Amberson's tutelage, though he insisted the money wasn't any cleaner than the stuff he used to make from the infamous Bugs Moran. And he found he had an equal talent for fixing up old houses. Crystal Latour's old town house began to shine.

Even the glowering assembled Emersons were powerless against Jamey's determination and charm. Particularly when Helen seemed so happy, how could they begrudge the mysterious upstart who suddenly appeared in their lives?

Ricky Drago's death was never fully explained, but then, as the state attorney said, who the hell cared? He'd come to a bad end, but one he more than deserved. May God have mercy on his soul.

As for Rafferty, it was all astonishingly clear. He'd spent thirty-four years of his life, sixty-four years of his nebulous afterlife, looking for someone to love him enough to save him. What he'd never realized was that he was the one who needed to find love. Not in another person, but within himself. It was his love for Helen that had saved him. And given him a lifetime of Valentines.

Including the first and most precious. Ms. Annabelle Emerson Rafferty was born at 3:35 a.m. on the morning of February 14. And big, bold, brave, bad Jamey Rafferty was there, holding Helen's hand for labor and delivery, longing for the days when all a father had to do was pace and smoke.

And he only passed out once.

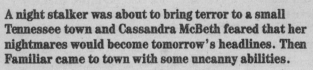

OFFICIAL RULES • MILLION DOLLAR BIG BUCKS SWEEPSTAKES
NO PURCHASE OR OBLIGATION NECESSARY TO ENTER

To enter, follow the directions published. **ALTERNATE MEANS OF ENTRY:** Hand print your name and address on a 3″ ×5″ card and mail to either: Harlequin "Big Bucks," 3010 Walden Ave., P.O. Box 1867, Buffalo, NY 14269-1867, or Harlequin "Big Bucks," P.O. Box 609, Fort Erie, Ontario L2A 5X3, and we will assign your Sweepstakes numbers. (Limit: one entry per envelope.) For eligibility, entries must be received no later than March 31, 1994. No responsibility is assumed for lost, late or misdirected entries.

Upon receipt of entry, Sweepstakes numbers will be assigned. To determine winners, Sweepstakes numbers will be compared against a list of randomly preselected prizewinning numbers. In the event all prizes are not claimed via the return of prizewinning numbers, random drawings will be held from among all other entries received to award unclaimed prizes.

Prizewinners will be determined no later than May 30, 1994. Selection of winning numbers and random drawings are under the supervision of D.L. Blair, Inc., an independent judging organization, whose decisions are final. One prize to a family or organization. No substitution will be made for any prize, except as offered. Taxes and duties on all prizes are the sole responsibility of winners. Winners will be notified by mail. Chances of winning are determined by the number of entries distributed and received.

Sweepstakes open to persons 18 years of age or older, except employees and immediate family members of Torstar Corporation, D.L. Blair, Inc., their affiliates, subsidiaries and all other agencies, entities and persons connected with the use, marketing or conduct of this Sweepstakes. All applicable laws and regulations apply. Sweepstakes offer void wherever prohibited by law. Any litigation within the province of Quebec respecting the conduct and awarding of a prize in this Sweepstakes must be submitted to the Régies des Loteries et Courses du Quebec. In order to win a prize, residents of Canada will be required to correctly answer a time-limited arithmetical skill-testing question. Values of all prizes are in U.S. currency.

Winners of major prizes will be obligated to sign and return an affidavit of eligibility and release of liability within 30 days of notification. In the event of non-compliance within this time period, prize may be awarded to an alternate winner. Any prize or prize notification returned as undeliverable will result in the awarding of that prize to an alternate winner. By acceptance of their prize, winners consent to use of their names, photographs or other likenesses for purposes of advertising, trade and promotion on behalf of Torstar Corporation without further compensation, unless prohibited by law.

This Sweepstakes is presented by Torstar Corporation, its subsidiaries and affiliates in conjunction with book, merchandise and/or product offerings. Prizes are as follows: Grand Prize—$1,000,000 (payable at $33,333.33 a year for 30 years). First through Sixth Prizes may be presented in different creative executions, each with the following approximate values: First Prize—$35,000; Second Prize—$10,000; 2 Third Prizes—$5,000 each; 5 Fourth Prizes—$1,000 each; 10 Fifth Prizes—$250 each; 1,000 Sixth Prizes—$100 each. Prizewinners will have the opportunity of selecting any prize offered for that level. A travel-prize option, if offered and selected by winner, must be completed within 12 months of selection and is subject to hotel and flight accommodations availability. Torstar Corporation may present this Sweepstakes utilizing names other than Million Dollar Sweepstakes. For a current list of all prize options offered within prize levels and all names the Sweepstakes may utilize, send a self-addressed, stamped envelope (WA residents need not affix return postage) to: Million Dollar Sweepstakes Prize Options/Names, P.O. Box 4710, Blair, NE 68009.

The Extra Bonus Prize will be awarded in a random drawing to be conducted no later than May 30, 1994 from among all entries received. To qualify, entries must be received by March 31, 1994 and comply with published directions. No purchase necessary. For complete rules, send a self-addressed, stamped envelope (WA residents need not affix return postage) to: Extra Bonus Prize Rules, P.O. Box 4600, Blair, NE 68009.

For a list of prizewinners (available after July 31, 1994) send a separate, stamped, self-addressed envelope to: Million Dollar Sweepstakes Winners, P.O. Box 4728, Blair, NE 68009.   SWP-H393

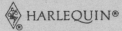